The
LUCY DANIELS
CAT
COMPANION

The

LUCY DANIELS

CAT

COMPANION

*Hodder
Children's
Books*

A division of Hodder Headline Limited

Special thanks to Narinder Dhami for *Cat Crazy*
Special thanks to Jill Atkins for *Ginger* and *Amber* (Nine Lives)
Special thanks to Heather Maisner for *Weed* (Nine Lives)
Special thanks to Jenny Oldfield for *Kitten in the Cold*, and
Chris Hall, B.Vet, Med, MRCVS for reviewing the veterinary
information contained in this book.

Contents

LUCY DANIELS
Cat Crazy

Illustrated by Paul Howard

To Billy, a very special kitten, much missed.

1

'Mandy Hope, I shouldn't think you can eat one more thing!' laughed Mrs Hope, as Mandy opened the cake tin. 'You and James have both eaten enough to feed an army!'

Mandy grinned at her mother. 'I was just wondering if there were any of those raisin scones left,' she said.

'Can I have one too, please?' asked James eagerly. He was lying on the picnic blanket with his Labrador puppy, Blackie, curled up beside him.

'There's just one.' Mandy held up the scone. 'We'll share it.'

Blackie woofed hopefully.

'OK, Blackie.' Mandy smiled at the puppy, who was wagging his tail like a little black flag. 'We'll all share it!'

Mr Hope shook his head. 'I've never seen two children and one young dog eat quite so much in my life!' he said to Mrs Hope.

'I always seem to get hungrier on holiday!' said James with a grin. 'And so does Blackie!'

The Hopes, Mandy's best friend, James Hunter, and, of course, Blackie, were on holiday for two weeks in an area of the Gloucestershire countryside called the Cotswolds. Mandy and James hadn't been to the Cotswolds before, and they were enjoying walking and cycling around the gently rolling hills and valleys. They weren't staying in one place, but were driving to a different pretty Cotswold village every few days.

Yesterday they had arrived at their last stop, a small bed-and-breakfast hotel in a village called Bilbury. Today was Wednesday, and Mandy and James were determined to make the most of the last few days of the holiday, before they went home on Sunday morning.

'I think this is the best holiday I've ever had,' Mandy said happily, as she fed Blackie a tiny piece of scone. 'I'm so glad we came!'

'I'm really glad you asked Blackie and me to

come too,' said James. 'Blackie's been quite good, hasn't he?'

They all looked at Blackie, who was sitting very still and staring hopefully at the scone Mandy was eating.

'He always is when there's food around!' Mandy laughed. She loved being on holiday with James and his dog. It was almost as good as having a pet of her own.

Mandy's parents were both vets, and worked in a surgery built on to the back of their house in the village of Welford. Because the surgery was always so busy with other people's animals, Mandy couldn't have a pet of her own, and it was difficult for Mr and Mrs Hope to take a holiday. But this time they'd managed to find another vet, Alison Morgan, to stand in for them.

'Wouldn't it be great if we could have brought all the animals from Animal Ark on holiday with us?' said Mandy with a grin. 'I wonder how they all are?'

Mr Hope laughed. 'I don't think there would have been room in the car for the rest of us!'

Mrs Hope put her arm round Mandy. 'We'll ring Alison tonight, and find out how everyone is getting on,' she promised.

James grinned. 'Mandy doesn't forget about animals even on holiday.'

'Of course I don't!' said Mandy. 'And talking of animals, it's about time we took Blackie for a walk.'

Blackie opened his eyes, and pricked up his ears at the word 'walk'.

James jumped up. 'All right,' he said. 'But I've eaten so much, I can hardly move!'

'You'd better keep Blackie on his lead,' said Mr Hope. 'We don't want him taking a dip in the river.'

Mandy bent down, and clipped the lead firmly to Blackie's collar. 'We'd never get him out again!' she said. Although she and James had been trying to train Blackie for months, he still didn't always do as he was told. 'Ready, James?'

James nodded.

'Don't be too long,' Mrs Hope called after them, as they set off along the river-bank.

'Look, James!' Mandy said, pointing at the water. 'Aren't the dragonflies beautiful?'

They stopped to watch the dragonflies skimming over the surface of the river for a few minutes. But Blackie was soon tugging at the lead, so they walked on.

Mandy smiled. She loved having Blackie around, and James didn't mind sharing him at all. She bent down to stroke the puppy, then handed the lead to James. 'Here, it's your turn.'

'Maybe we'd better go back now,' said James, winding Blackie's lead firmly round his hand. 'Your mum said not to go too far.'

'Lazybones!' Mandy teased him. 'We'll just go round the next bend of the river. Then we'll turn back.'

James nodded. 'OK. But next time we have a picnic, remind me not to eat so much!'

They carried on along the bank. The river twisted and turned in a long curve, and Mandy and James followed its path.

There were some ducks swimming in the water, and Blackie began to bark as soon as he spotted them. The ducks swam off as fast as they could.

'He won't hurt you,' James called. 'He just wants to make friends, that's all.' He turned to Mandy with a grin, as the ducks scuttled off in all directions. 'I don't think they believe me!'

But Mandy wasn't listening. She grabbed James's arm, and pointed at something ahead of them. 'Look, James!'

There was a black cat sitting on the river-bank. It was having a wash, and licking its leg with its pink tongue.

'Hello, puss!' said James, as the cat stopped washing, and stared curiously at them.

'Isn't it gorgeous!' Mandy said. 'Let's go and make friends.'

'What about Blackie?' James asked, looking down at his puppy, who was sniffing around in the grass. 'It might not like dogs.'

Just then Blackie noticed the cat, and pricked up his ears. He was used to cats because James had one called Benji, but he always got excited when he saw one. He started barking loudly. The black cat looked alarmed, and jumped to its feet.

'Quiet, Blackie!' James gasped, trying to stop himself from being dragged along the river-bank. 'You'll frighten it!'

Mandy frowned. 'Look, James,' she said in a worried voice. 'I think it's hurt!'

James stared at the little black cat. He could

see what Mandy meant. One of its front legs didn't look quite right. The cat was holding it awkwardly across the other one, so that its front paws were crossed. 'What's wrong with it?' he asked anxiously.

Mandy was staring hard at the cat. 'I don't know,' she said. 'But we can't just leave it here if it's hurt.'

Mandy began to walk slowly towards the cat, holding her hand out in front of her. The cat watched her with big green eyes. It didn't look scared at all. It started to walk towards her, limping heavily on its front leg.

Quickly Mandy knelt down, and held out her hand close to the cat's face. For a moment, the cat didn't do anything. Then it sniffed Mandy's hand, and let her stroke its head.

'Can you see what's wrong with its leg?' James called. He tied Blackie to a nearby tree, and went over to stroke the cat himself. 'Do you think it was hit by a car?'

Mandy shook her head. 'There's no blood,' she said, puzzled. 'I think it may be an old injury.'

'You mean it was hurt somehow, and left with a limp?' James looked upset. 'That's awful.'

'I wonder where it's come from,' Mandy said, tickling the little cat's tummy. 'Maybe it lives in the village.'

They could just see the village where they were staying, through the trees that grew along the river-bank. But it seemed a very long way for a little cat with a bad leg to walk.

Mandy looked worried. 'I hope it isn't lost,' she said.

'Maybe we ought to take it back to your mum and dad,' James suggested. But, right at that moment, the little cat got up and started to limp away in the other direction.

'We'd better follow, and make sure it's all right,' Mandy decided quickly.

James went to get Blackie, and they all hurried after the little cat. The cat looked over its shoulder and saw them following, but didn't seem to mind.

'We'd better not go too far,' James said nervously. 'Your mum and dad will be wondering where we are.'

Mandy didn't answer. Instead she nudged James in the ribs, and pointed down the river-bank.

'Wow!' she gasped. 'Look at that!'

2

'It's a boat full of cats!' said James, his eyes wide with amazement.

The boat was a long, thin barge, the kind of boat that people sometimes live in, instead of a house. It was painted in reds and blues, and there was a picture of a black-and-white cat painted on the side. Above that, the name of the boat was written in red letters – *The Puss-in-Boat*.

There was a coal-black cat, a marmalade cat and a tabby cat asleep on top of the cabin, all curled up together. Two black-and-white cats were eating from food bowls on the boat deck, and Mandy and James counted another six cats walking up and down, or sitting washing themselves. As they stared in amazement, the little black cat jumped gracefully from the river-bank on to the deck. Then she sat down to have another wash.

'*The Puss-in-Boat*,' said James, with a grin. 'I can see why it's called that!'

'Me too!' Mandy agreed, her eyes shining. She'd never seen so many cats all together in one place before. 'Let's go a bit closer.'

Mandy, James and Blackie hurried along the river-bank until they reached the barge. As they got closer, they could see that the boat was quite shabby, and needed a new coat of paint. But there were pots of flowers on the deck, and all the cats looked healthy and well fed.

'How many cats are there?' James asked in a dazed voice.

'Well, I can see twelve,' said Mandy, as a big orange-and-white cat padded round from the other side of the boat. 'No, thirteen.'

'Did you count the grey one near the flowers?' James asked, pointing it out.

Mandy couldn't remember, so they had to start counting all over again. Meanwhile, the little black cat was sniffing round the empty food bowls. When she realised there was no food left, she began to miaow loudly.

'Who looks after all these cats?' James wondered.

Mandy was still counting under her breath. 'Oh no, now I've lost count again!' she sighed. 'How many do you make it, James?'

'Eighteen,' said someone else's voice.

A fair-haired boy of about Mandy's age had appeared from below the deck, and was smiling shyly at them. Mandy and James smiled back.

'Come on board and say hello to our cats,' the boy said. 'Mum won't mind, will you, Mum?'

A young woman in denim dungarees, with the same colour hair as the boy, followed him on to the deck. She waved at Mandy and James. 'Hello. I'm Lucy Browne, and this is my son, Martin. Do you like cats?'

'We're Mandy Hope and James Hunter,' Mandy said, 'and we love cats.'

'Well, do come and meet ours. We're always looking for volunteers to give them a cuddle.' Lucy grinned at them. 'It isn't easy finding the time to give eighteen cats all the love and attention they need!'

Mandy and James were thrilled. James tied Blackie to the nearest tree, and they stepped on to the barge. Blackie looked a bit disappointed for a moment. Then he lay down, put his nose between his paws and went to sleep.

As soon as Mandy and James were aboard, they were surrounded by cats. Mandy scooped up the

nearest one into her arms, and he snuggled down
on her shoulder. He was a big marmalade cat,
and he had the loudest purr Mandy had ever
heard.

'That's Pusskin,' said Lucy. 'He's our oldest cat.
He's fifteen.'

Mandy gave Pusskin a cuddle. He purred even
louder, and put his paws round her neck. Mandy
didn't want to put him down, but there were so
many other cats begging for attention that she had
to. She knelt down and stroked as many as she
could, trying hard to remember all their names.

James was holding a beautiful tabby, with big

green eyes and an orange mark on her forehead. 'What's this one called?' he asked.

'That's Penny,' said Martin. 'She catches anything that moves.'

'And leaves it on the deck for us to trip over next morning!' added Lucy.

'Why do you have so many cats?' Mandy asked curiously, stroking Lily, a black cat with glossy fur.

'Well, first of all, we had three cats of our own,' Lucy began. 'Then we took in a few strays, and people started bringing us more and more,' she explained. 'Three of the cats were left homeless when their elderly owners died. I didn't have the heart to turn any of them away.'

'Some of them have been badly treated,' said Martin. He pointed to a very strange-looking cat who was asleep in a shady corner of the deck. 'Like Muffin.'

'Poor thing,' said James. 'He looks as if most of his fur has been shaved off.'

'The vet had to do that,' said Lucy. 'Muffin's a Persian cat, and their fur has to be brushed regularly or it gets all tangled up.'

'You mean his owner didn't look after him properly?' Mandy asked indignantly. She hated it when people couldn't be bothered to look after their pets.

Lucy nodded. 'Muffin's fur was such a mess, we couldn't brush it,' she said. 'But it'll grow back.'

There was suddenly a loud *miaow* behind them. They all jumped, and turned round. The little black cat was still sitting by the empty food bowl.

Lucy laughed. 'I think you've met Queenie, haven't you?'

'Yes.' Mandy knelt down, and stroked her. 'She's gorgeous! But what happened to her leg?'

'She got knocked down by a car,' said Lucy. 'And her owner didn't want her back, because her leg never healed properly.'

'That's terrible!' said Mandy.

Queenie miaowed again at the top of her voice, and Lucy covered her ears. 'She won't stop until we feed her,' she laughed.

'I'll feed her,' Martin offered. 'I think Effie needs feeding too.'

'Who's Effie?' James asked.

Lucy smiled. 'She's the newest addition to our family – and she produced four babies almost as soon as she arrived here!'

'Kittens!' said Mandy, her face lighting up. 'Where are they?'

'Below deck,' said Martin, pointing at the cabin door.

'All tucked up in a basket with their mum!'

Lucy added. 'They're only three weeks old.'

'Where did Effie come from?' James asked.

'Mrs Cox, who runs the village post office, found her wandering about, and brought her to us,' Lucy explained. 'She would have loved to keep the cat herself, but she's got two dogs already.'

'And we've taken in a couple of other cats from the village,' Martin added. 'Smokey was a stray that old Mr Tilbury brought to us, and Lily belonged to a family who were going to live abroad and couldn't take her with them.'

'Can we see the kittens now?' Mandy asked eagerly.

'Of course, if you have time,' said Lucy with a smile.

Mandy and James looked at each other, remembering they'd promised not to be away too long on their walk.

'My mum and dad will be waiting for us just down the river-bank,' Mandy said reluctantly. She was longing to see the kittens, and there were still some cats she hadn't said hello to yet, but they couldn't keep her parents waiting much longer.

'Well, why don't you ask them if they'd like to come to *The Puss-in-Boat* for a cup of tea?' suggested Lucy. 'Then they can meet the cats, and the kittens too.'

Mandy's eyes lit up. 'That would be brilliant!' she said. 'Come on, James. Let's go and tell them.'

Mandy and James stepped over the cats still milling around their feet, and climbed off the barge.

'We'll be back soon, we hope!' Mandy called, waving at their new friends. James untied Blackie, and then the three of them ran back along the river-bank the way they'd come.

'There you are!' said Mrs Hope, as Mandy, James and Blackie raced up to them. 'We were beginning to wonder where you were.'

'Oh, we've had a brilliant time!' Mandy gasped. 'We went on this barge, and we saw lots of cats!'

'Eighteen cats!' added James. 'And Lucy and Martin look after them, and they've invited us all for tea!'

Mr and Mrs Hope looked puzzled. 'Could one of you take a deep breath, and go through that again?' asked Mr Hope.

So Mandy told them the whole story.

'It sounds as if Lucy and her son are doing a very good job, looking after all those cats,' said Mrs Hope. 'We'd love to come and see them.'

'Great!' Mandy jumped to her feet. 'Can we go right now?'

'Your mum and I had better pack the picnic things away first,' said Mr Hope, picking up the basket. 'You go on ahead, and tell Lucy and Martin that we're on our way.'

'OK!' Mandy and James were already off, running along the river-bank with Blackie bounding along beside them.

'The boat's called *The Puss-in-Boat*,' Mandy shouted over her shoulder. 'You can't miss it!'

'No, I don't suppose there are many boats with eighteen cats!' Mr Hope called back.

'Aren't Lucy and Martin great?' Mandy said to James, as they raced along the river-bank. 'I don't know what would have happened to those cats if they hadn't taken them in.'

'I know,' James replied. 'How can people be so horrible?'

'At least the cats are safe on *The Puss-in-Boat* now,' said Mandy.

They followed the bend in the river, and there was the barge, bobbing gently on the water.

'Look, there's Lucy,' said James. 'She's talking to someone.'

Lucy was standing on the river-bank with a man and a woman. As Mandy and James got nearer, they could see that the man's face was red, as if he was cross about something.

'This isn't good enough, young lady,' they heard the man say in an angry voice. 'I'm going to see to it that all these cats are removed, as soon as I possibly can!'

3

Mandy and James jerked to a halt on the river-bank, and looked at each other in horror. What on earth was going on?

'Mr Pengelly,' Lucy was saying politely, 'the cats really aren't doing any harm—'

'Well, I found one in my garden the other day, and the day before that!' Mr Pengelly said angrily. He was a small, round man with grey hair and a grey beard. 'It's not right keeping so many animals on a boat – it's a health hazard!'

'Why don't you come on to *The Puss-in-Boat* and have a cup of tea?' Lucy suggested. 'Then we can have a chat.'

Mr Pengelly shook his head. 'I'm warning you,' he said furiously. 'No one in the village wants you here, and we're taking steps to have you moved on! Come along, Marjorie.'

Mr Pengelly marched off, and the woman, who hadn't said a word, followed him. Lucy looked very upset, and so did Martin, who was standing on the barge. James quickly secured Blackie, while Mandy rushed up to Lucy.

'Who were those horrible people?' she asked indignantly.

Lucy sighed. 'That's Mr Pengelly and his wife,' she said. 'They live in the village, and he's been

complaining about us ever since we arrived here five weeks ago.'

'Why?' James asked.

'He says the cats are a nuisance, and they go in his garden,' Martin replied.

Lucy frowned. 'I don't understand it,' she said. 'Most of the cats are so nervous, they never go as far as the village. They stay close to the boat.'

'Doesn't he know you're looking after cats that have been badly treated?' Mandy asked. 'Maybe if Mr Pengelly knew that, he might calm down a bit.'

Lucy managed a smile. 'He never gives me a chance to get a word in edgeways! But I don't think it would make any difference anyway.'

'He wants us to move the boat on somewhere else,' added Martin, 'but we can't, can we, Mum? The engine needs repairing.'

Lucy nodded. 'We only just managed to get it this far,' she said. 'If we're forced to go, we'll have to leave the boat behind and move into a flat, and then, of course, we won't be able to take all the cats with us.'

'There must be something we can do,' Mandy said desperately. 'Maybe we could help you find homes for them.'

'We're always trying to find good homes.' Martin bent down to stroke Penny. 'But most people don't want older cats.'

'Well, let's have tea, and we can talk about it later.' Lucy smiled at Mandy and James. 'Come on to the boat, and I'll put the kettle on.'

Mandy and James looked at each other as they followed Lucy on to *The Puss-in-Boat*. If only there was something that she and James could do to help, Mandy thought. But what?

As before, Mandy and James were surrounded by cats as soon as they reached the deck of the boat. But this time Mandy noticed how many other cats *didn't* come out to be fussed and stroked. There were some who stayed back, hiding themselves away and looking fearfully at Mandy and James. Mandy guessed that these were the animals who had been treated so badly. They were scared of humans they didn't know. What would happen to these cats if Lucy and Martin had to leave *The Puss-in-Boat*?

'Here are your mum and dad, Mandy,' said James. In the distance they could see Mr and Mrs Hope walking along the river-bank, carrying the picnic basket.

Mandy turned to Lucy and Martin. 'My mum and dad are both vets,' she said. 'I could ask if they would check over all the cats for you, if you like. If the cats are healthy, then maybe that horrible man won't have so much to complain about.'

Lucy's face lit up. 'That would be wonderful,' she said. 'At the moment I have to take the cats to an RSPCA clinic, and it's miles away from here.'

Mr and Mrs Hope were getting closer now, so Mandy and James scrambled off the boat, and ran to meet them.

'Dad!' Mandy gasped. 'There's this horrible man called Mr Pen-something—'

'Pengelly,' said James.

'And he's trying to get rid of *The Puss-in-Boat*!' Mandy continued breathlessly. 'And Lucy and Martin might have to move into a flat—'

'And they won't be able to take the cats with them,' James finished off.

Mr Hope held up his hand. 'Hold on a minute, you two! Let's say hello to your new friends first, before you tell us exactly what's going on.'

'Come on then, Dad!' said Mandy eagerly. She grabbed her father's hand, and started tugging him towards the barge, where Lucy and Martin were waving at them.

'Maybe Lucy and Martin would like us to give the cats a quick check-up while we're here,' Mrs Hope suggested as they walked up to the boat. 'It can't be easy looking after so many cats.'

'Oh, thanks, Mum!' said Mandy. 'I hoped you'd say that!'

Lucy and Martin were waiting for them on the

deck, as they climbed aboard.

'Hello,' said Lucy. 'Welcome to *The Puss-in-Boat!*'

'Hello.' Mrs Hope smiled, as she looked round. 'What a wonderful name for a boat full of cats!'

Lucy and Martin looked pleased. For the next few minutes, everyone was busy chatting, and stroking all the cats who curled around their ankles, and jumped up on to their laps.

'Would you like to look round the boat before we have tea?' Lucy asked.

Mandy's eyes lit up. At last she was going to see the kittens!

The Puss-in-Boat wasn't very big, but everything was neat and tidy. Lucy and Martin took their visitors all round the deck, and then to the rooms below. The two bedrooms, kitchen and bathroom were narrow and cramped, but everything was clean.

'Oh, who painted these?' asked Mandy. She'd just spotted some water-colour paintings of cats pinned to the cabin walls.

'I did,' said Lucy. 'I sell them to raise money to look after us and the cats.'

'They're lovely!' said Mandy. She pointed to one of the paintings. 'That's Pusskin, isn't it?'

'And that's Queenie!' said James. Lucy had painted Queenie, the little black cat with the limp, sitting with her injured leg crossed over the other, just as she'd done when Mandy and James first saw her.

The kittens and their mother were in a basket, under a low, narrow table. Mandy waited impatiently as Lucy knelt down, and gently pulled the basket into view. Five sleepy faces looked up at them. Effie, the mother, was black and white, and so were the kittens, although their markings were all different.

'Oh, they're gorgeous!' Mandy said softly.

Lucy had warned them that Effie was quite a nervous cat, so they all stayed still and quiet, as she lifted the kittens gently out of the basket. She put the biggest one into Mandy's arms.

'This one's called Button,' she said. 'The others are Candy, Snoopy and Joe.'

Even though Button was the biggest of the four, he was still tiny. He was black all over, except for his white socks. Button looked up at Mandy and miaowed.

'He's lovely!' Mandy said happily, rubbing her cheek against the kitten's soft fur.

They played with the kittens for a while, and then they all went back on deck, and had tea and biscuits. As they were finishing their tea, Mr Hope turned to Lucy. 'Mandy and James were saying you've been having problems with someone from the village.'

Lucy quickly explained about Mr Pengelly. 'We've only been here a little while,' she said, 'but he took a dislike to us from the start.'

Mr Hope frowned. 'I think Mr Pengelly's being a little unfair,' he said. He put out his hand, and scooped up the cat nearest to him. 'Shall we start checking the cats over now? I think I recognise this one from Lucy's picture!'

'That's Queenie,' said Mandy. 'She's the one who brought us here!'

Mr Hope gave Queenie a quick check-up. 'Well, you'll be glad to know that, apart from her leg, she seems to be very healthy. Now, who's next?'

Everyone helped to bring the cats to Mr and Mrs Hope to be checked over. But some of the cats didn't want to be checked over at all.

'Come out, Smokey!' gasped Martin. Some of the cats had gone below deck to hide, and Martin was flat on his tummy, trying to coax Smokey out from under one of the beds. 'No one's going to hurt you.'

Mandy came down from the deck to see what was going on. 'I don't think she believes you!' she said. 'Maybe you could get her out with some food?'

'Good idea,' said Martin. 'She loves cheese. I'll go and get some.'

Martin managed to get Smokey out with a small

piece of cheese. Almost all the cats had been checked over by now. Apart from Pusskin, whose sore eye Lucy had already noticed, the cats seemed to be in the best of health.

'Is that all of them?' Mandy asked. There were so many cats, it was impossible for her to keep count.

Lucy frowned. 'I think there's just Jessie left. She's another of our nervous ones, and she's probably hidden herself away.'

'What does she look like?' Mandy asked.

'She's black and white.' Lucy smiled. 'And she's easy to recognise, because she's much too fat!'

Mandy wandered round the deck, keeping a sharp look-out for Jessie. Then she spotted her. The small, round cat had wedged herself into a tiny gap between two lifebelts.

'Come on, Jessie,' Mandy murmured gently. She knelt down and held out her hand. But to her amazement, the cat put out its paw, and slapped her hand away.

Mandy jumped. She wasn't hurt, because the cat hadn't put its claws out. She was just surprised. She put out her hand again, and again the cat slapped it away.

Lucy saw what was happening, and came over. 'Jessie used to belong to a family who teased her all the time,' she said quietly, as she knelt down

by Mandy. 'And now, if she's scared, she hits out at people with her paw.'

Mandy felt very upset. The cat looked so unhappy. 'Will she come out for you?' she asked.

'She might,' Lucy replied. She knelt down, and, after a few minutes, she managed to get Jessie out to be checked over.

'Pusskin's eye infection should clear up in a couple of days, if you carry on bathing it,' said Mr Hope, as he put his jacket back on. 'It isn't serious.'

'Thank you so much,' said Lucy gratefully. 'I was going to take him to the RSPCA clinic tomorrow, so you've saved me a trip.'

'How long are you staying in the village?' Martin asked, as the Hopes and James got ready to leave.

'Until Sunday,' said Mrs Hope. She looked at Mandy and James, who were saying goodbye to all the cats. 'So I don't think you've seen the last of us!'

'Oh, please come and see us whenever you like!' said Lucy. 'What about tomorrow morning?'

'We'd love to!' said Mandy eagerly.

They left the boat, waving to Lucy and Martin and the cats, and began the walk back to the village.

Mandy couldn't stop thinking about Jessie and Smokey, who were so scared and unhappy. She turned to James. 'We can't let Mr Pengelly force Lucy and Martin to abandon *The Puss-in-Boat*!'

'That's just what I was thinking!' James said. 'But what can we do?'

'I don't know yet,' said Mandy. Then she added, in her most determined voice, 'But we'll have to think of something!'

4

Thursday morning was bright and sunny. Mandy and James were up early and, because it wasn't time for breakfast yet, they took Blackie out into the garden behind the hotel.

'I dreamt about cats all night!' James said with a grin.

'So did I!' said Mandy. 'I can't wait to go back to *The Puss-in-Boat* today.'

'Me too,' James agreed. Then he frowned. 'I hope Mr Pengelly doesn't turn up though.'

Mandy sighed. 'I just wish he would give Lucy and Martin a chance,' she said. 'What on earth is going to happen to all the cats if they have to leave the boat?'

James looked worried. 'Have you come up with any brilliant ideas about how we can help them?'

Mandy shook her head. 'Not really.' Then she smiled. 'But remember Tibby's six kittens? We found a good home for them, didn't we?'

James nodded, looking more cheerful. 'Yes, we did!' But then his face fell again. 'That was back home in Welford, though. It's different here. We don't know anybody.'

Mandy knew what James meant. They couldn't just walk up to people they didn't know, and ask them if they wanted a cat. And, as Martin had said yesterday, older cats were a lot more difficult to find homes for than kittens. 'We'll just have to do our very best,' she said firmly.

'Yes, we will,' James agreed. Then he looked round. 'Oh no! Blackie! Stop that!' he shouted.

Blackie was having a lovely time digging a hole in one of the flowerbeds, and sending earth flying everywhere. James raced over, and dragged the puppy out.

'Bad dog, Blackie!' he gasped, pointing sternly at the Labrador. Blackie just wagged his tail, and jumped up to lick James's hand.

'Good morning, you two.' Mrs Ross, the owner of the small bed-and-breakfast hotel, opened the door, and came out into the garden.

She was a round woman with greying hair, and a warm smile. As soon as Blackie saw Mrs Ross, he pulled away from James and bounded up to her, wagging his tail. 'And how's Blackie this morning?'

'Just as naughty as usual,' said James. 'I'm sorry, Mrs Ross, but he's dug a hole in one of your flowerbeds.'

'Oh, don't worry about that,' said Mrs Ross with a smile, as she bent down to stroke the excited young dog. 'It doesn't look like there's any serious damage done. Now, are you ready for breakfast?'

'Yes, please,' James said eagerly.

'Well, why don't I give Blackie *his* breakfast, while you two go and wash your hands?' Mrs Ross suggested, with a twinkle in her eye. 'I'm sure he's hungry after all that digging!'

'Thanks, Mrs Ross,' James said gratefully, as she took Blackie indoors.

Mandy looked thoughtful as they washed their hands in the cloakroom. 'I wonder what Mrs Ross thinks about *The Puss-in-Boat*,' she said, as she reached for the soap. 'Mr Pengelly said that no one in the village wants *The Puss-in-Boat* here. But perhaps some people don't feel like that. Mrs Cox, for instance: she asked Lucy to take in Effie, didn't she?'

'Yes,' said James. 'And I bet Mrs Ross doesn't mind *The Puss-in-Boat*. She loves animals.'

'There aren't many hotels that let you bring your pet on holiday with you,' Mandy agreed.

James grinned. 'Especially pets like Blackie!'

Mr and Mrs Hope were already sitting at the breakfast table in the dining-room when Mandy and James hurried in.

'Hello, you two.' Mrs Hope smiled at them. 'Do you want cereal?'

'Yes, please,' Mandy said. 'We're starving!'

'What a surprise!' Mr Hope laughed as he passed James the cornflakes box. 'So, I expect you two would like to go back to *The Puss-in-Boat* this morning, wouldn't you?'

Mandy nodded eagerly. 'Lucy said we could.'

'All right,' Mrs Hope said, with a smile. 'We'll take you there after we've finished breakfast. Your dad and I have decided to go for a long walk this morning.'

Mrs Ross came in just then, carrying a large tray loaded with tea and toast. She brought it over to their table.

'Here we are, then.' She beamed at them. 'There's scrambled eggs, bacon and sausages coming in just a moment, and I've fed Blackie too. Goodness me, James, that dog of yours can eat!'

James grinned. 'I know,' he said. 'Eating and misbehaving are Blackie's two favourite things!'

'So what are you all planning to do today then?' Mrs Ross asked, as she set out the teacups.

'James and I are going to *The Puss-in-Boat* to see Lucy and Martin and their cats,' said Mandy. 'Do you know them, Mrs Ross?'

'Yes, I do.' Suddenly Mrs Ross looked sad. 'Lucy and Martin helped me to look for my cat when he went missing a few weeks ago. I don't know what I'd have done without them.'

'I didn't know you had a cat, Mrs Ross,' Mandy said.

'Poor William was too ill to make it home on his own,' Mrs Ross sighed, looking even more upset. 'He died a few days later. He was sixteen years old, so he'd had a good life. I miss him, though.'

Mandy bit her lip. 'I'm sorry, Mrs Ross.'

Mrs Ross smiled at her a bit tearfully, and then began to bustle round the table, pouring out the tea. 'Well, anyway, Lucy and young Martin seem very nice.'

'They are,' said James.

'They're doing a good job of looking after all those cats too,' remarked Mr Hope. 'But we've heard that some people in the village aren't happy about them being here.'

Mrs Ross frowned. 'That's true enough,' she said. 'There are some villagers who think that the cats are a nuisance, and that the boat's too small to have so many cats on it.'

'It's very clean though,' Mandy pointed out, 'and so are the cats.'

Mrs Ross nodded. 'But I think some people are worried that Lucy might carry on taking in more and more strays. I suppose they're concerned that the village might be overrun with cats.' She finished pouring out the tea. 'Still, Lucy was very helpful to me. And I know for a fact that she looked after Miss Dawson's cat, when the old lady had to go into hospital for a few days.'

Mandy was pleased. It looked like there were several people who wouldn't support Mr Pengelly. She wondered if Mrs Ross had heard about his threat to get rid of *The Puss-in-Boat*.

'Do you know Mr Pengelly, Mrs Ross?' she asked.

'Oh, yes, dear.' Mrs Ross frowned. 'I've heard he's not happy about *The Puss-in-Boat* at all.'

'No, he isn't,' said James. 'We saw him there yesterday.'

Mrs Ross shook her head. 'I wouldn't worry about Harry Pengelly,' she said comfortingly. 'He's not a bad person, but he's always got a bee in his bonnet about something. Now, I'd better get back to my kitchen, or there'll be no scrambled eggs for you today!'

Mandy frowned as Mrs Ross went out. In spite of what the hotel owner had said, she was still worried. Mrs Ross might not take any notice of Mr Pengelly, but other people in the village might.

After breakfast, they all set off for *The Puss-in-Boat*. While Mandy and James were with Lucy and Martin, Mr and Mrs Hope were going to take Blackie with them on their country walk.

The sun was getting warmer now, and there wasn't a cloud in the deep-blue sky.

Mandy and James ran eagerly on ahead, along the river-bank, with Blackie running beside them. They raced round the bend in the river. Lucy was standing on the deck of *The Puss-in-Boat*. They waved at her.

'We'll say a quick hello, and then we'll be off,' said Mr Hope, as he and Mrs Hope caught up.

They all went over to *The Puss-in-Boat*. Lucy was still on deck, but Mandy couldn't see Martin anywhere.

'Hello, Lucy,' called Mrs Hope.

Lucy hurried across the deck of the barge

towards them. 'Hello, how lovely to see you all again.'

'We're off on a walk,' said Mr Hope. 'We'll be back for Mandy and James in a couple of hours, if that's all right?'

'That's fine,' said Lucy.

Mandy and James climbed on to *The Puss-in-Boat*.

'Bye then, you two,' called Mrs Hope as she, Mr Hope and Blackie turned to leave. 'Be good!'

'We will!' Mandy called back.

'Mum?' Martin suddenly appeared from below deck. He looked worried. 'I can't find her. She isn't in the cabin.' Then he saw Mandy and James. 'Oh, hi there.'

'Hello, Martin.' Mandy looked puzzled. 'Have you lost one of the cats?'

'It's Queenie,' Martin said miserably. 'We've looked all over the boat, and she isn't here.'

'We haven't seen her since last night,' Lucy added, looking worried. 'She's never been gone this long before.'

'We'll help you look for her, won't we, Mandy?' James offered.

'Of course we will,' Mandy said. She couldn't bear to think of the little cat with its injured leg lost somewhere, cold and hungry. 'Let's start right away!'

5

'What about looking for Queenie along the river-bank?' Mandy suggested. 'That's where James and I first saw her.'

'Good idea,' said Lucy. 'If you, Martin and James go one way, I'll go the other.'

They all climbed off the barge, and on to the river-bank.

'Now don't go too far,' Lucy called after them, as they set off.

Mandy, Martin and James walked slowly along, calling Queenie's name. They searched the hedgerows along the river-bank, but couldn't find Queenie anywhere. They went on until they had followed the path round the bend in the river.

'I think we'd better go back,' Martin said.

Mandy stared along the river-bank. There was no sign of the little black cat anywhere. 'Where can she be?' she asked miserably, as they started back towards the boat.

'You don't think she might have fallen into the river, do you?' asked James.

Martin shook his head. 'Queenie hates the water. She won't go anywhere near it.'

'All cats are like that, aren't they?' said James.

Martin smiled. 'Not all of them,' he said. 'We used to have a cat called Victor who loved swimming!'

Mandy thought hard for a minute. 'Do you think Queenie might have gone to the village?' she suggested.

'She might have done,' Martin said. 'Let's go and see if Mum has had any luck.'

They got back to *The Puss-in-Boat* just a few minutes before Lucy came hurrying towards them from the opposite direction. Mandy, James and Martin were waiting eagerly for her, but their faces fell when they saw that she was alone.

'Mandy suggested looking in the village, Mum,' said Martin.

Lucy nodded. 'It's a good idea. Let's go.'

Lucy and Martin knew a footpath which took

a short cut across the fields, and was much quicker than going by road.

The village was small and very pretty, with its old stone church and winding streets full of thatched cottages. They stopped by the churchyard, and Lucy turned to the others.

'I think we'd better split up again,' she said. 'I'll go this way.' She pointed down the hill. 'You three can look round the houses behind the church.'

Mandy, James and Martin nodded.

'I'll meet you back here in ten minutes,' Lucy called over her shoulder as she set off. 'Don't be late!'

'Maybe we ought to look for Queenie in the churchyard too,' Mandy suggested. 'There are lots of places she could be hiding.'

But Queenie wasn't in the churchyard.

Behind the church was a row of thatched cottages. All of the cottages had large front gardens filled with brightly-coloured flowers and shrubs. Mandy, James and Martin began to walk along the road, staring into all the gardens.

'I've just remembered who lives in one of these cottages,' Martin said suddenly.

'Who?' asked James.

'Mr Pengelly!' Martin looked worried. 'I hope Queenie isn't in his garden!'

Mandy frowned. 'So do I!'

'Mr Pengelly said he'd found a cat from *The Puss-in-Boat* in his garden,' James remembered. 'But he didn't say which one.'

'Which house is the Pengellys', Martin?' Mandy asked anxiously.

Martin pointed to the next house in the row. 'Number Eight.'

They stopped outside the gate, and glanced quickly round the front garden. Mandy felt very nervous indeed.

'I don't think Queenie's here,' Martin said, sounding relieved.

'No,' Mandy said. 'Thank goodness!'

'Just a minute,' James said suddenly. 'Something just moved, over there in the flowerbed!'

Martin and Mandy looked where James was pointing, and Mandy's heart sank. There was Queenie, sitting under a large shrub, having a wash. After a few seconds, she started to settle down, looking as if she'd found the perfect spot for a nap.

'We've got to get her out,' Mandy said desperately, 'before Mr Pengelly sees her!'

'Queenie!' Martin called softly.

Queenie opened her big green eyes, and peered out through the leaves. She saw Martin and miaowed a greeting. Then she

yawned, and closed her eyes again.

'Queenie!' Martin whispered again, but the cat took no notice.

'She's too sleepy to move,' Mandy said urgently. 'We'll have to go and get her ourselves!'

Martin was already unlatching the gate. 'I'll be as quick as I can,' he whispered. 'Let's hope no one sees us!'

He hurried into Mr Pengelly's garden, dashed over to the flowerbed, and scooped Queenie up into his arms. Queenie was surprised, but then she snuggled down on Martin's shoulder, and began to purr.

'Now get out of there!' Mandy said breathlessly.

But just then they heard the sound of a door opening. With sinking hearts, Mandy, James and Martin looked towards the house.

Mr Pengelly was standing on his doorstep, with a shopping bag in his hand, staring in amazement. 'And just *what* do you think you're doing in my garden?'

6

For a moment or two, the three of them were too shocked to say anything. Then Mandy stepped forward. 'We're very sorry, Mr Pengelly,' she said in a wobbly voice. 'We didn't mean any harm. Martin had to get his cat back, that's all.'

Mr Pengelly looked at Queenie, and frowned. 'That cat is always coming into my garden!' he said angrily. 'I've had enough of this!'

'What on earth is going on?'

Everyone looked round. Lucy was hurrying towards them, looking worried.

'Mum!' Martin rushed over, and put Queenie

into her arms. 'We found Queenie in Mr Pengelly's garden.'

'Yes, and I came out and found your son in here without my permission!' snapped Mr Pengelly.

'Oh dear!' said Lucy.

'Sorry, Mr Pengelly,' said Martin.

The old man frowned. 'This is just what I've been complaining about, Miss Browne!' he snapped. 'That cat keeps coming into my garden, and digging up my flowerbeds—'

'She wasn't doing any harm,' Martin argued. 'She was just asleep.'

Mr Pengelly looked even more annoyed. 'That's all very well, but what if she starts encouraging your other cats to come and sleep in my garden? I'm not having it!'

Mandy got a sudden picture in her mind of Queenie leading all the other cats from *The Puss-in-Boat* in a long line into Mr Pengelly's garden. It was such a funny thought that she wanted to laugh, but she didn't dare, because he looked so angry.

'I can't understand why Queenie would come into your garden, and no one else's,' Lucy was saying. 'No one else has complained.'

'Well, what are you going to do about it?' Mr Pengelly folded his arms, and glared at them.

'We'll keep an eye on Queenie, and try to make sure she doesn't go far from the boat,' Lucy promised.

Mandy frowned. That wouldn't be easy. It was practically impossible to keep cats in one place, without locking them up.

Mr Pengelly shook his head. 'I'm afraid that's not good enough, Miss Browne. I've decided to start a petition to get you and your boat moved on, and I'm going to get everyone in the village to sign it!'

'A petition!' Mandy gasped. She looked at Martin and James in horror. Things were going from bad to worse.

'Please, Mr Pengelly,' said Lucy. 'Can't we talk about this?'

'There's nothing to talk about,' said the old man, and he marched off down the street.

'What an awful man!' said James indignantly.

Lucy sighed. 'I don't think he's being very fair,' she said. 'But Queenie was in his garden, after all.'

'How many people do you think will sign the petition, Lucy?' Mandy asked anxiously.

'I don't know,' Lucy replied. 'I haven't had any other complaints, so maybe he won't get many.' But she didn't sound too sure.

'Mrs Ross won't sign it,' said James.

'No, I'm sure she won't,' Mandy agreed. But she was very worried about how many other people in the village would.

Lucy managed a smile. 'Well, that's one person on our side, anyway! Come on, let's go back to *The Puss-in-Boat*.'

They set off back to the barge.

'Shall I carry Queenie for a bit?' Mandy asked Lucy. 'Your arms must be tired.'

'Thanks, Mandy,' Lucy replied gratefully. She gave Queenie to Mandy, and the little black cat settled herself down on Mandy's shoulder. She seemed to be enjoying the ride.

As she walked along, stroking Queenie's warm

fur, Mandy thought hard about what she and James could do to help Lucy and Martin and the cats. They couldn't just let Mr Pengelly go ahead with his petition, and force *The Puss-in-Boat* to leave, or close down. They had to fight back. But how?

'Mandy?'

Mandy was thinking so hard that she didn't realise James was speaking to her. Then she blinked. 'Sorry, James. What did you say?'

'Queenie's gone to sleep on your shoulder!' James grinned at her. 'She must be tired out after all that excitement!'

Mandy gently hugged the little cat, and Queenie started to purr sleepily. 'I was just thinking about Mr Pengelly,' Mandy said. 'If he's going to start a petition, then we have to do something too.'

'But what?' asked Martin.

Mandy frowned. 'I'm sure if everyone in the village knew the good job that *The Puss-in-Boat* was doing, they wouldn't sign the petition.'

'Do the people in the village know all about the cats?' James asked Lucy and Martin, as they walked along the river-bank.

Lucy shrugged. 'Well, I suppose some of them do,' she said. 'I've helped a few people out when they needed their cats looking after or re-housed, but we don't know that many people in the village.'

James looked at Martin. 'Haven't you made any friends here yet?'

Martin shook his head. 'We got here too late for me to start at the village school last term,' he said. 'I was going to go there after the holidays. But now it doesn't look like we'll be here . . .' His voice trailed away.

They were close to *The Puss-in-Boat* now. Penny and Pusskin, who were sitting on the river-bank, saw them, and came to meet them.

James knelt down to stroke the two cats. 'It's such a shame,' he sighed. 'If only everyone in the village could come and see the cats and get to know them, I'm sure they wouldn't sign Mr Pengelly's petition.'

Mandy gasped, and her face lit up. 'James!' she said softly. 'You're a genius!'

James looked puzzled. 'I am?' he said, pushing his glasses up his nose.

'Lucy,' Mandy said, her voice trembling with excitement. 'What about having an Open Day?'

'An Open Day?' Lucy repeated.

'Yes, so that everyone in the village can come along and visit *The Puss-in-Boat*!' Mandy explained breathlessly. 'Then they can meet the cats, and see how well you look after them!'

'Oh, Mandy, what a brilliant idea!' said Lucy, a huge smile spreading across her face.

Mandy turned pink. 'Well, it was James's idea really,' she pointed out.

'No, the Open Day was your idea, and I think it's great!' said James enthusiastically.

'So do I,' Martin added.

Mandy looked pleased. 'We can make some posters to advertise it,' she said, thinking hard, 'and put them up around the village. We want everyone to come.'

'Even Mr and Mrs Pengelly?' asked James.

'*Especially* them!' Mandy said firmly. 'And we could put out deckchairs and tables, and sell refreshments. What do you think, Lucy?'

Lucy nodded. 'It's a good idea. But we can't have too many people on the barge at one time, though. There isn't room, and it wouldn't be safe.'

'We could put the table and chairs on the river-bank, next to the barge,' James suggested. 'And we could decorate the boat with balloons and streamers.'

'That would be lovely,' Lucy agreed. 'And I could bake a few cakes and biscuits to sell.'

'And we could sell cups of tea and coffee, and lemonade,' James said eagerly.

'Maybe you could sell some of your paintings as well, Mum,' Martin suggested.

'Why not?' Lucy agreed, as they all climbed aboard the barge. 'We might even make some money for repairs!'

'Oh, I hope so!' said Mandy. Then, even if Lucy and Martin had to move on, at least they wouldn't have to give up the boat, and leave the cats behind.

'When shall we hold the Open Day?' asked Martin.

Lucy thought for a minute. 'We'll have it on Saturday afternoon, the day before Mandy and James leave.'

'But will we have enough time to get everything ready?' Mandy asked anxiously.

'Of course we will!' said Lucy. 'Anyway, we can't have the Open Day without you two. After all, it was your idea!' She put her arm round Mandy's shoulder, which woke Queenie up. She opened her eyes, and miaowed grumpily.

'Don't worry, Queenie!' laughed Mandy. 'You can be the star of the Open Day!'

'We'd better get started on some posters right away,' said Lucy. 'We need to let everyone in the village know about the Open Day, and we don't have much time.'

Mandy nodded. She was determined to make the Open Day a big success. *The Puss-in-Boat* was depending on them.

7

Mandy, James and Martin were sitting on the grassy river-bank, paper and paints spread out all around them.

'How are you getting on?' called Lucy. She was sitting on the deck of the barge, making a list of all the things they needed for Saturday afternoon.

Mandy held up her poster for Lucy to see. 'Open Day at *The Puss-In-Boat*!' it read in large, colourful letters, and she had drawn a black cat underneath the words. 'That's supposed to be Queenie,' she said, frowning at her drawing. 'But I don't think it looks much like her!'

James and Martin were also hard at work. James's poster read:

Are you CAT CRAZY?
Then why not come to the Open Day
at *The Puss-in-Boat*!
This Saturday at 2 o'clock.

'I think I'll draw a picture of the barge at the bottom,' James decided.

Martin had written the same words as James in the middle of his poster, and now he was drawing a border of cats all round the edge of the paper.

'Make sure the posters are really bold and bright!' Lucy called from the barge. 'We've got to make people notice them!'

'Hello, everyone!'

They all looked round. Mr and Mrs Hope and Blackie were walking along the river-bank towards them.

'Mum! Dad!' Mandy jumped to her feet, and raced to meet them. James and Martin followed her. Blackie saw them, and began to bark joyfully.

'Did you have a good walk?' James asked, as Blackie hurled himself into his arms.

'Yes, thank you, James,' said Mr Hope.

'And what have you three been up to?' asked Mrs Hope curiously. She could see that Mandy,

James and Martin were all nearly bursting with excitement.

Mandy explained about the Open Day.

'What a good idea!' said Mrs Hope. 'We'll help, won't we, Adam?'

'Of course,' said Mr Hope with a smile. 'Just tell us what you want us to do.'

'Thank you,' said Lucy gratefully, as she climbed off the boat to join them. 'But we don't want to spoil your holiday. And, anyway, there isn't much to do until Saturday.'

'We're all going out tomorrow,' said Mrs Hope.

Mandy suddenly remembered that the next day they were going to visit an old friend of her father's, Roger Thomas, who ran a wildlife hospital not far from Bilbury. She had been really looking forward to it, but with the excitement of the Open Day, she had forgotten all about it. Still, as Lucy had said, once the posters were up, there wasn't much more they could do until the actual afternoon of the Open Day arrived.

Lucy asked Mr and Mrs Hope on to the barge for a cup of tea, but they said no thank you, as they were dirty and muddy, and really needed to go back to the bed and breakfast to change their clothes.

'I can drop Mandy and James off at the bed and breakfast when we've finished putting up the

posters, if you like,' Lucy suggested.

'Thank you,' Mrs Hope said. 'That would save us a trip back here to collect them.'

'We'll see you all in an hour or two, then,' called Mr Hope, as he and Mrs Hope carried on along the river-bank with Blackie.

Mandy, James and Martin continued with their posters, while Lucy went back to her list.

Mandy finished first. She rolled the poster up carefully, and put it with the others they had already made. They would have six posters to put up around the village. Soon everyone would know all about the Open Day.

Mandy wondered nervously how many villagers would actually come along. Mr Pengelly wouldn't, she thought, her heart sinking. But Mrs Ross had said that Mr Pengelly wasn't a bad person. Maybe he would give *The Puss-in-Boat* another chance, if they could just make him see how important it was . . .

Mandy had an idea. She picked up a piece of paper, folded it in two to make a card and began to draw on the front of it.

'What are you doing?' asked Martin.

'Just wait and see,' Mandy said mysteriously.

James and Martin looked at each other. 'I think she's up to something,' said James. 'Mandy always has a scheme.'

When the posters were finished, they all set off for the village to put them up. They stopped near the churchyard gate. Just to the side of the gate, there was a large noticeboard with a couple of posters, one about a village barn dance and another giving the times of the church services.

'I'll ask the vicar if I can put one on the noticeboard here,' Lucy decided, taking three posters from Martin. 'And one could go outside the school, and another outside the village hall.'

'We could put one on the community noticeboard on the green,' Martin suggested. 'Lots of people would see it there.'

'And we could ask Mrs Ross to put one in the window of the bed and breakfast,' James added.

'Good idea,' said Lucy. 'Then we'll only have one left. Where can we put it?'

'I know!' Mandy said suddenly. 'What about the post office? I'm sure Mrs Cox wouldn't mind. After all, you helped her out by taking Effie and her kittens in.'

'That's a brilliant idea!' said Martin. 'Lots of people go to the post office every day.'

Lucy went to find the vicar. Meanwhile, Mandy, James and Martin walked on to the village green, and stopped at the community noticeboard. There wasn't anything on it except a poster about a mother and baby group at the church hall. Carefully Martin unrolled one of their posters, and pinned it in the middle of the board. They all stood back to admire it.

'Now the post office,' said Martin. 'It's just across the green.'

James and Martin set off across the grass, but the lace on one of Mandy's trainers had come undone, so she knelt down to re-tie it. As she did so, two women carrying shopping baskets stopped by the noticeboard.

'Look at that, Betty,' said one of them, a short woman with dark hair. 'There's an Open Day on Saturday, on that boat – the one with all the cats.'

'You know I can't stand cats, Vera,' said her friend. She was taller than the first woman, and

wore large, horn-rimmed glasses. 'Nasty, dirty creatures they are.'

Mandy's heart sank as she tied up her lace. She hoped there weren't too many other people in the village who shared this view.

'I found my dustbin lid knocked off again this morning, and there was rubbish all over my garden path,' Betty went on. 'I bet it was those dratted cats.'

'It could have been a fox, Betty,' Vera pointed out quickly. 'I quite like cats myself, you know. We used to have a lovely tabby called George years ago.'

'I hear Harry Pengelly's getting up a petition to have that boat moved on,' Betty remarked, as the two women walked on. 'I've a jolly good mind to sign it.'

'Oh, but I don't think they're doing any harm,' Vera argued. 'I might pop along to this Open Day myself, just to see what's going on . . .'

As Mandy ran to catch up with James and Martin, she couldn't help worrying about how many people in the village would agree with Mr Pengelly and Betty about the cats. They wouldn't know for sure, though, until the afternoon of the Open Day itself. It all depended on how many people bothered to turn up. Betty's friend hadn't sounded too sure about whether she was going to come or not. What if no one came at all?

Mandy decided not to tell James and Martin what the two women had said as she caught up with them outside the post office. There was no point in them *all* worrying.

'Let's go and see Mrs Cox,' said Martin.

They were about to go into the post office when the door opened and Mrs Ross came out.

'Hello, Mrs Ross,' James said. 'We were coming to see you later!'

Mrs Ross looked puzzled. 'Whatever for?' she asked curiously.

Quickly Mandy explained about the Open Day. 'And we were wondering if you would put up a poster in the window of the bed and breakfast,' she finished.

Mrs Ross beamed at them. 'What a wonderful idea!' she said. 'And of course I'll put a poster up! But I hope you'll let me help out a little more than that.'

'Yes, please!' said Mandy eagerly.

'Well, for one thing I have lots of deckchairs and garden tables you can borrow.' Mrs Ross smiled at them. 'I keep them for my guests, so I've got a lot more than most people.'

'Thanks, Mrs Ross!' said James.

'And I could do a bit of baking for the refreshment stall,' Mrs Ross added. 'How about that?'

'That would be wonderful,' said Martin gratefully.

'It's the least I can do after you and your mum helped me find my William,' said Mrs Ross. She took one of the posters, and then hurried off down the road, turning back to wave at them.

'Isn't she nice?' said Mandy, as they went into the post office.

James nodded. 'I hope she makes some of her raisin scones!' he said.

The post office was empty, except for Mrs Cox, who was sitting behind the counter, reading a magazine. She was a tall, thin woman, with an untidy bun of grey hair and round glasses.

'Hello, Martin,' she said warmly. 'How are you? And how are the kittens and their mum?'

'They're fine, Mrs Cox,' said Martin.

'I'm glad to hear it,' said the postmistress. 'Now, what can I get for you and your friends?'

Martin gave her one of their posters. 'We were wondering if you'd put this up in your window,' he said.

Mrs Cox unrolled the poster and looked at it. 'Of course I will!' she said. 'What a good idea! I'm sure lots of people in the village will come.'

'We hope so,' said Mandy.

The door opened and Lucy came in. 'Hello, Mrs Cox,' she said, then she turned to Mandy,

Martin and James. 'I've put all the posters up.'

'So have we,' said James.

'If you want to borrow any deckchairs, Lucy, I've got some in my garden,' Mrs Cox offered, 'and I can let you have some paper plates and plastic cups.'

'Oh, thank you, Mrs Cox!' said Lucy gratefully.

'Mrs Ross is lending us some chairs and tables too,' said Mandy, 'and she's going to bake some refreshments.'

'Everyone's being so kind,' said Lucy. 'I just hope the cats appreciate it!'

'Of course they will!' said Mandy.

'Martin and I will walk you two back to the bed and breakfast now,' said Lucy, glancing at her watch. 'Come on.'

They said goodbye to Mrs Cox and went out. Mandy was feeling quite cheerful again now. As Lucy had pointed out, most people were being very helpful about the Open Day. Mandy was beginning to think that it couldn't possibly fail . . .

But there was a nasty shock waiting for them outside the post office. Mr Pengelly was standing there, holding a clipboard, and talking to a large man who wore a flat cap.

'. . . and this petition is to try and get that boatful of cats moved on,' Mr Pengelly was saying, as he showed the man the papers he was holding. 'As you can see, I've got some signatures already.'

Mandy was horrified. Mr Pengelly hadn't wasted any time starting up his petition. How many signatures had he got already? A lot or just a few? As they walked by, Mandy tried to sneak a look at the clipboard he was holding, but she couldn't see. Mr Pengelly didn't notice them going by. He was too busy talking to the man in the flat cap.

'I'll sign it,' Mandy heard the man say as they

walked on. 'My dustbin lid was knocked off again this morning, and there was rubbish all over my lawn. I'm fed up with it.'

'It's not fair!' Mandy burst out as soon as they were out of earshot. 'It could easily be a fox that's raiding the dustbins!'

Lucy nodded. 'Maybe we could ask if anyone in the village has seen foxes around at night.'

'I wonder how many people have signed Mr Pengelly's petition,' James said anxiously.

Nobody answered, but everyone looked miserable. Then Mandy remembered the card she had made when they were designing the posters. She had slipped it into her pocket, and forgotten about it. 'Before we go to the bed and breakfast, can we go to Mr Pengelly's house?' she asked Lucy.

'Mr *Pengelly*'s house?' Martin and James said together, staring at Mandy in amazement. Lucy looked surprised too.

Mandy took a deep breath. She was feeling a bit silly now, but it was too late to get out of it. So she took the card she had made out of her pocket.

'I've made a special invitation for Mr and Mrs Pengelly,' she explained. 'I thought that maybe then they might come to the Open Day.'

James looked doubtful. 'I don't think they will.'

Martin shook his head. 'Me neither.'

'Well, at least they can't say they haven't been invited!' Mandy said stubbornly.

'I think it's a very nice thought,' Lucy agreed.

They walked to Mr Pengelly's house. While the others waited at the gate, Mandy went up the path, and pushed the invitation through the letterbox. Then, as she turned to leave, she noticed something very odd indeed. There was a dustbin near the front door. The bin was very full, so the lid didn't fit properly, and through the gap, Mandy could see what looked like the edge of an empty cat food tin.

Cat food? Mandy frowned. The Pengellys didn't have a cat. So why was there an empty cat food tin in their dustbin?

8

'Well,' said Mr Hope as he turned the Land-rover down the road that led back to Bilbury, 'I think we all enjoyed that!'

'I did!' said Mandy eagerly. 'The fox cubs were gorgeous!'

It was the following afternoon, and the Hopes and James had just returned from visiting Roger Thomas, Mr Hope's friend. They had set out after breakfast, and had soon arrived at the wildlife hospital, which wasn't far away. The hospital was a long bungalow with large grounds in the middle of the countryside.

As soon as Mr Hope pulled up outside the

building, Roger Thomas, a cheery-looking man with dark hair, came out to meet them.

'Adam! Emily!' he called. 'Great to see you!' Roger welcomed Mandy and James too. 'I've heard you both quite like animals?' he went on, with a twinkle in his eyes.

'We *love* animals!' said Mandy eagerly. She could hardly wait to see what kind of animals were being cared for at the hospital.

'Then you've come to the right place!' said Roger. 'Come on, I'll give you the guided tour.'

The hospital was looking after all sorts of sick wild animals. There was a young deer with a broken leg, two owls with injured wings, and several hedgehogs amongst the many patients. There were also two fox cubs, who had lost their mother.

Mandy gave a gasp of delight when she saw them. 'They're gorgeous!' she said softly, stroking their russet-coloured heads.

'They're due for a feed soon,' Roger told her. 'You can help the nurse give them their milk if you like.'

Mandy and James were thrilled. Roger gave each of them a cub to hold while the nurse fetched the bottles of milk. The cubs were lively and inquisitive, and one of them even tried to go head first down James's sweatshirt. But as soon as the milk arrived the cubs settled down for their feed.

'It's a bit like feeding a baby!' Mandy laughed, as the cubs drained their bottles right down to the last drop.

After helping to feed the fox cubs Mandy and James joined Roger and Mr and Mrs Hope for a delicious lunch, before heading back to Bilbury.

Mandy had been so interested in the wildlife hospital and its patients, especially the fox cubs, that she had forgotten about *The Puss-in-Boat* for a little while. But now, as they drove into the village, she started wondering what had been happening while they had been away. Had Mr Pengelly been out collecting more signatures for his petition?

'Look!' said James suddenly. 'There are Lucy and Martin!'

Lucy and Martin were walking up the high street, carrying bags of shopping. Mr Hope tooted the horn, and then pulled into the kerb.

'Hello,' called Mrs Hope, winding down the window. 'How are you both?'

'All right, thank you,' said Lucy, although Mandy thought both she and Martin looked a bit depressed. 'We've been to buy decorations and drinks for tomorrow.'

'And we met Mr Pengelly,' Martin added. 'You'll never guess what he's done!'

'What?' asked Mandy.

'He's called a meeting in the village hall on Monday night to discuss *The Puss-in-Boat*!' Lucy told them worriedly.

'Oh no!' Mandy exclaimed.

'At least Mr Pengelly's meeting is after the Open Day,' James said. 'Maybe by then we'll have enough people on our side.'

'I hope so,' Lucy sighed. Then she looked up at the sky, and groaned. 'Oh, no, it's starting to rain! That's all we need!'

Mandy's heart sank as big drops of rain began to splash on to the Land-rover's windscreen. Who would bother to come to the Open Day in weather like this?

'Can we give you a lift?' asked Mr Hope.

Lucy shook her head. 'Thanks, but we've got more shopping to do.'

'We'll see you tomorrow morning then,' said Mrs Hope.

They waved goodbye to Lucy and Martin, and Mr Hope drove on. Mandy gazed miserably up at the grey sky as the rain grew heavier. At this rate, it looked as if the Open Day was doomed before it had even started!

9

As soon as Mandy opened her eyes on Saturday morning, she jumped out of bed and hurried over to the window. She pulled the curtains back, and looked eagerly outside. Her face fell. The sky was grey and overcast. Still, at least it wasn't raining, she thought, trying to be cheerful.

The Open Day was scheduled to start at two o'clock, and there was a lot of work to be done before then. After breakfast, Mandy and James helped Mr and Mrs Hope pack the Land-rover with deckchairs and tables. Mrs Cox had given them a big silver urn to boil water for tea and coffee, as well as packets of plastic cups and cutlery, and paper plates.

'At least that means there won't be any washing-up to do when the Open Day's over!' Mrs Hope said, looking relieved.

At last everything was packed tightly in, and Mr Hope closed the doors. 'We'll see you at *The Puss-in-Boat!*' he called, and drove off with Mrs Hope. Mandy and James had promised to help Mrs Ross pack up and deliver the cakes she had baked for the Open Day, so they hurried back into the bed and breakfast to find her.

'I can't wait for it to start,' James said eagerly as they went towards the kitchen.

'Me too.' But Mandy couldn't help sounding a bit worried, and James frowned. 'Are you all right, Mandy?' he asked.

Mandy nodded. 'It's just – well, what if no one turns up?'

'Of course people will turn up,' James said confidently. 'No one would miss out on a great day like this!'

Mandy managed a smile. 'I suppose not,' she said, as she knocked at the kitchen door.

'Come in,' Mrs Ross called.

Mandy and James opened the door, and walked in. Their eyes grew wide with amazement. Lined up on the kitchen counter were four large, delicious-looking cakes, along with three plates piled with scones and biscuits, and a plate of jam tarts.

'Do you think that will be enough?' Mrs Ross asked. 'I didn't have time to make any more.'

'Mrs Ross, it's brilliant!' Mandy said, her eyes shining. Then she looked more closely at the plate of gingerbread biscuits, and began to laugh. 'Oh, James, look!'

Instead of gingerbread men, Mrs Ross had made gingerbread cats, with curly tails and currants for eyes. Mandy and James were thrilled.

'I've had that cat-shaped biscuit cutter for years and never used it,' Mrs Ross said, beaming at them. 'I thought today was the *purr*-fect time to try it out!'

Mandy and James groaned at the joke. They helped Mrs Ross pack the cakes carefully into boxes, then they set off to walk to *The Puss-in-Boat*.

As they passed the poster they had stuck up on the community noticeboard, Mandy wondered again how many people had seen the posters and decided to come along. Well, she wouldn't have to wait long to find out.

They turned down into the road where the Pengellys lived.

'I hope we don't meet Mr Pengelly!' James whispered in Mandy's ear. But there was no one around except for a milkman, standing next to his milk float, talking to a woman. It wasn't until they got closer that Mandy saw it was Mrs Pengelly.

'And I'll have an extra pint of milk, please,' Mrs Pengelly was saying.

The milkman smiled. 'That makes three extra pints this week!' he said. 'Someone's drinking a lot of milk in your house!'

He took three bottles from the float, and handed them to Mrs Pengelly, who hurried back into the cottage.

'Do you know Mrs Pengelly?' Mandy asked Mrs Ross.

'Not very well,' Mrs Ross replied. 'She keeps herself to herself. She doesn't say much.'

'Mr Pengelly doesn't give anyone a chance to say anything!' James pointed out.

Mrs Ross smiled. 'Well, let's hope he calms down a bit and comes to the Open Day,' she said.

They took the short cut to the river across the fields. As they got closer to the barge, they could see that everyone was busy. Mr Hope was setting out the tables and chairs on the river-bank, Mrs Hope and Lucy were standing on stepladders hanging streamers and balloons in the trees, and Martin was unpacking the plastic cups.

James went to help Martin, and Mrs Ross and Mandy began to set up the refreshments stall.

'Mrs Ross, you're a marvel!' Lucy exclaimed, as they unpacked all the cakes, biscuits and scones. 'Thank you so much for doing all this.'

'It's a pleasure,' said Mrs Ross. 'After all, you helped me when I needed it.'

Mandy tried not to keep worrying, but she couldn't help it. Would it rain? The sky still looked grey, although it was a little brighter than when she had woken up that morning. What if Mr Pengelly had already turned most of the villagers against the barge?

Mandy hoped desperately that the Open Day would be a success. She couldn't bear to think what would happen to *The Puss-in-Boat*'s cats if it wasn't.

It was almost two o'clock. In a few minutes the Open Day was due to start, and Mandy stood on the river-bank, looking round. The boat looked wonderful with its balloons and streamers, and with Lucy's cat paintings displayed all over the cabin. The nearby trees were decorated too. Some of the cats were lying around on the boat deck, and some were strolling on the river-bank, weaving their way between the tables and chairs. Mandy looked for Queenie, but couldn't see her.

Mrs Ross was behind the refreshments stall, which was laden with the cakes, scones and biscuits

that she and Lucy had baked. The hot water urn was steaming gently, ready for making tea and coffee, and bottles of lemonade were lined up next to the piles of plastic cups. Everything was ready.

'I think we're all set!' Lucy smiled. She put her arm round Mandy's shoulders. 'Now all we've got to do is wait for people to turn up!'

Mandy smiled back, even though her heart was pounding. Then, suddenly, James grabbed her arm.

'Look!' he said.

Mandy looked where James was pointing. There was a man, a woman and a little girl walking across the fields towards *The Puss-in-Boat*. Her face lit up. 'Are they coming here?'

'It looks like it,' Mr Hope said. 'We'd better start opening those bottles of lemonade!'

An hour or so later, Mandy couldn't even remember why she'd been so worried. There had been just a few visitors at first, and then more and more had arrived. Now the Open Day was in full swing.

Although the sky was still overcast, it hadn't rained, and now and then a gleam of pale sunshine broke through. There were people sitting around on the river-bank, chatting, drinking tea and lemonade and eating Mrs Ross's and Lucy's cakes.

Some of the visitors were holding cats in their

arms or on their laps. Mandy spotted Pusskin being petted by one man, and Penny in the arms of a little girl. Meanwhile, Mandy's parents were busy answering questions about pet care, and especially about looking after cats. James and Martin had made a big sign reading 'ASK THE VET', and there was a long line of people queuing to speak to Mr and Mrs Hope.

Lucy was on the deck of *The Puss-in-Boat*, and people were going on board to see for themselves where the cats lived, as well as to look at Lucy's paintings. Mandy could see that she'd already sold a few of them.

The only thing that wasn't so good was that Mr and Mrs Pengelly hadn't come, after all. Mandy sighed. She hadn't really thought that her invitation would do the trick, but she couldn't help hoping . . .

'Mandy!' Lucy hurried over to her. 'Isn't this wonderful? Everything's going so well!'

Mandy grinned at her.

'I've sold four cat paintings,' Lucy went on, 'and two other people have asked me if I can do a portrait of their pets.'

'That's great!' Mandy said happily.

'But best of all, I think I might have found new homes for some of the cats!' Lucy beamed at her. 'I've got homes for all the kittens, as soon as

they're old enough. Someone has asked me about adopting Lily, and another lady wants Muffin. Oh, and Mrs Ross is having Pusskin!'

That was the best news of all! To know that some of the cats would be going to loving homes was the best reward for all their hard work.

'Goodness me!' Lucy said suddenly, sounding very surprised. 'Here come Mr and Mrs Pengelly! I never expected to see them!'

Mandy's face lit up. Mr and Mrs Pengelly had come to the Open Day! Maybe her special invitation had done the trick after all! But when she looked over at the Pengellys, she wasn't so sure. Mr Pengelly was marching along the river-bank with a large cardboard box in his arms, looking very red in the face. Mrs Pengelly was hurrying along behind him, and she looked rather red too.

Mandy felt her heart sink. The Open Day had been going so well. Had Mr and Mrs Pengelly come to spoil it?

10

Just at that moment, Mr Pengelly spotted Lucy and Mandy. He headed straight towards them, looking very angry indeed. Mrs Pengelly scurried along behind him.

'Hello, Mr Pengelly,' Lucy said nervously. 'We're so glad you decided to come to the Open Day—'

'We're not here for the Open Day!' snapped Mr Pengelly. 'We're here to return this!'

He pulled open the box he was holding, and Queenie stuck her head out. She saw Lucy and Mandy and began to miaow loudly. Mandy bit her lip. It looked like the little cat had been caught in Mr Pengelly's garden once again.

'Oh, Queenie!' Lucy sighed, lifting the cat out of the box. 'Why can't you behave yourself?'

'I found her under my rosebush,' Mr Pengelly went on furiously. 'And I want to know what you're going to do about it!'

Lucy looked helplessly at him. 'I just don't know why Queenie keeps on going into your garden, Mr Pengelly. I'm very sorry.'

'That's not good enough!' snapped Mr Pengelly. 'And I'm not standing for it any longer!'

Mandy glanced at Mrs Pengelly to see what she thought. But Mrs Pengelly didn't look angry, she looked very embarrassed. Maybe she was just ashamed of Mr Pengelly for making a scene at the Open Day. Unless there was another reason . . .

Mandy remembered the empty tin of cat food she had seen in the Pengellys' dustbin, as well as the extra pints of milk Mrs Pengelly had bought from the milkman.

'Excuse me, Mr Pengelly,' she said slowly. 'I think I might know why Queenie keeps coming to your garden.'

Mr Pengelly stared at Mandy. 'What do you mean?'

'Well,' Mandy looked at Mrs Pengelly. 'Cats keep going back to a place if someone there is feeding them.'

Mrs Pengelly turned bright red.

'No one's feeding that cat at *my* house!' Mr Pengelly began crossly, but then his wife cleared her throat.

'Er – Harry,' she said quietly, 'I think it's time for me to own up.'

Mr Pengelly turned to stare at his wife.

'I've been feeding Queenie,' Mrs Pengelly said.

'*You?*' spluttered Mr Pengelly. 'But why?'

Mrs Pengelly smiled at her husband. 'Because she reminds me of our Sooty,' she said.

'Who's Sooty?' Mandy asked.

'The cat we had when we were first married,' Mrs Pengelly replied. She tickled Queenie under the chin. 'You remember our Sooty, don't you, Harry?'

Mr Pengelly stared hard at Queenie. 'I suppose she does look a bit like Sooty,' he muttered reluctantly.

'Sooty was such a lovely cat!' Mrs Pengelly went on. 'Do you remember how he sat on your lap for hours in the evenings? He was so fond of you, Harry!'

Mr Pengelly didn't say anything, but Mandy thought she saw him almost smile, even though he still looked embarrassed.

'We used to say that Sooty was the most handsome cat in town!' Mrs Pengelly smiled at

her husband. 'Well, Queenie's just as beautiful.'

She put out her hand, and gently stroked Queenie's head. The cat purred, and climbed into her arms. 'I'm sorry, Miss Browne.' Mrs Pengelly looked nervously at Lucy. 'I thought Queenie was a stray when I started feeding her. I've been feeling very guilty about getting you into trouble.'

'That's all right.' Lucy smiled at her. 'I'm glad we've got this sorted out!'

Mandy looked at Mr Pengelly. He didn't look angry any more, just very embarrassed. Mandy couldn't help feeling a bit sorry for him.

'I'm sorry, Miss Browne,' he muttered. 'Obviously I didn't know that my wife was – er – encouraging the cat to come into our garden.'

'Won't you both come and have some tea?' Lucy asked. 'Then you can see how careful we are to look after the cats properly.'

But Mr Pengelly shook his head. 'I've got to get back home,' he muttered. 'Got some jobs to do in the garden.'

'I'll stay for a little while,' said Mrs Pengelly. 'I'd like a cup of tea. And then I'd like to have a look around *The Puss-in-Boat*, if I may.'

Mr Pengelly hurried off, while his wife went over to the refreshments stall, still carrying Queenie in her arms.

Her eyes shining with relief, Lucy turned to

Mandy, and patted her on the back. 'Well done! How on earth did you work out that Mrs Pengelly was feeding Queenie?'

Mandy explained about the extra milk Mrs Pengelly was having delivered, and the cat food tin in the dustbin. 'But I didn't guess what they meant until I saw how embarrassed Mrs Pengelly looked,' she said.

'Well, let's hope that this will stop Mr Pengelly from causing further trouble for *The Puss-in-Boat*!' Lucy said happily.

James and Martin came running over, Blackie at their heels. 'What did Mr Pengelly want?' asked James.

Lucy smiled at the two boys. 'We'll tell you all about it,' she said. 'But first let's go over to the refreshments stall, because Mandy deserves a big slice of chocolate cake!'

Mandy turned pink with pleasure. The Open Day was turning out to be a success. Maybe now Mr Pengelly might drop his petition against *The Puss-in-Boat*, and cancel the meeting at the village hall. Then Lucy and Martin and the cats would be able to stay.

Mandy smiled as they went over to the refreshments stall. The Open Day had been hard work, but it had all been worth it to try to keep the cats safe.

★ ★ ★

The Open Day was so popular, it continued into the early evening. As soon as the last visitor had left, the Hopes, James, Lucy, Martin and Mrs Ross set to work tidying up, packing away the chairs and tables and picking up the litter. It was hard work, and they didn't finish until quite late.

'I think the Open Day has been the best part of the whole holiday!' James said with an enormous yawn.

'Well, I for one have never worked quite so hard on a holiday before!' Mr Hope replied with a smile. 'But it was definitely worth it.'

'We've raised such a lot of money!' Lucy said happily. 'I think we'll be able to start having the barge repaired quite soon!'

Mandy was delighted. That meant that even if Lucy and Martin did have to move on, at least they wouldn't have to leave the boat and the cats behind. If only Mr Pengelly would stop his campaign to get *The Puss-in-Boat* moved on, everything would be perfect. They would just have to wait and see what the old man decided to do next.

'I can't believe we're going home today!' Mandy sighed, as she, James, Mr and Mrs Hope and Blackie walked along the river-bank. 'I'm really going to miss *The Puss-in-Boat.*'

Mrs Hope put her arm round Mandy. 'We all will,' she said. 'But at least we've done our very best to help.'

Mandy nodded. It was Sunday morning, the day after the Open Day, and they were on their way to say goodbye to Lucy, Martin and the cats before they went back home to Welford.

When they arrived at *The Puss-in-Boat*, Martin was on the deck, feeding some of the cats. Lucy was down in the cabin, but she hurried out when they climbed aboard, Mr Hope carrying Blackie.

'Hello,' Lucy called. 'Are you ready to leave?'

'We'll be going in about an hour,' said Mrs Hope.

'And how's Pusskin settling in at the bed and breakfast?' asked Lucy.

'He loves it,' Mandy replied. 'He and Mrs Ross are great friends already.'

Martin came over to them, carrying Queenie. 'There's someone here who wants to say goodbye to you,' he said, and he put the black cat into Mandy's arms.

'Hello, Queenie!' said Mandy, stroking the cat's head. 'I'm going to miss you!'

'Me too,' said James. 'After all, she was the one who brought us here.'

'She's a very clever cat!' said Martin, tickling Queenie under the chin.

Mandy noticed a man coming across the fields towards the barge. She recognised him, and frowned. 'That's Mr Pengelly!' she said.

Lucy looked nervous. 'Oh dear!' she said. 'What does he want now?'

They all waited in silence as Mr Pengelly came up to the barge. Mandy's heart was in her mouth. Surely Mr Pengelly hadn't come to complain about something else?

Looking embarrassed, Mr Pengelly nodded good morning to everyone. Then he looked at Lucy. 'I'd like a word with you, Miss Browne, if I may.'

'Yes, of course,' Lucy said. 'Do come on board.'

Mr Pengelly climbed carefully on to the deck. 'My wife and I had a long talk yesterday, and . . .' Mr Pengelly stopped and cleared his throat, '. . . she tells me that your boat is very clean and tidy.' He glanced round the deck. 'And I can see for myself that she's right.'

Lucy smiled. 'Thank you.'

'I want you to know that I've called off my – er – campaign to have you and your cats moved on,' Mr Pengelly muttered. 'I won't be going ahead with the petition or the meeting.'

Mandy and James grinned at each other. *The Puss-in-Boat* was safe!

'There's just one more thing.' Mr Pengelly looked even more embarrassed. 'My wife's very upset at the thought of Queenie not coming round any more.' He looked at Queenie, who was still in Mandy's arms. 'So I was wondering if we could – er – keep her?'

Mandy could hardly believe her ears. 'You mean you want to adopt her?'

Mr Pengelly nodded. 'If that's all right?' He looked at Lucy.

'Perfectly all right!' said Lucy cheerfully. 'I think you and Mrs Pengelly will give Queenie a wonderful home! We'll bring her round to you later on today if you like.'

Mr Pengelly nodded, turning even redder. He said a hasty thank you and goodbye, patted Queenie quickly on the head and hurried away.

'Well!' said James. 'Mrs Ross said Mr Pengelly wasn't a bad person, and she was right!'

'That's four cats who have found homes now, as well as all the kittens,' Mandy said.

'Five,' said Martin. 'The vicar came to see us this morning. He wants to adopt Penny. He's got mice in the vicarage!'

'I'm so glad we can stay!' Lucy said joyfully. 'We've made some good friends here, and Martin

will be able to go to the village school.'

Mandy grinned. Even she could hardly believe how well things had turned out.

'Time for us to be going,' said Mr Hope, glancing at his watch.

'Goodbye, Queenie,' said Mandy, and she gave the cat a final hug.

'Goodbye, Queenie,' said James, doing the same. 'We won't forget you!'

'And we won't forget you!' said Lucy. 'These are just to say thank you for all your help!' She held up two small water-colour pictures of a black cat, and gave one each to Mandy and James.

'It's Queenie!' James said. 'Thanks!'

'Thank you very much!' Mandy added, her eyes shining with delight. The paintings would be the perfect reminder of a *purr*-fect summer holiday!

LUCY DANIELS
Kitten in the Cold

Illustrated by Shelagh McNicholas

To the real Amber

1

'Mandy, are you sure you know what you're doing?' Grandad Hope asked as she lifted Smoky on to the kitchen table at Lilac Cottage.

Gran tut-tutted. 'For goodness' sake, Tom, you can see that the cat is in good hands. Stop fretting and let Mandy get on with it.' She bustled to fetch a small bottle of cleanser, a bowl of hot water and some cotton wool.

'We'll need a towel,' Mandy warned. 'Smoky won't like having his ears cleaned. He'll try to shake his head. The cleanser gets everywhere.'

Grandad brought a striped red towel and spread it on the table. 'That stuff's not too hot, is it?'

Mandy dipped the bottle into the hot water, while Smoky strolled up and down to investigate.

'Tom!' Gran said. 'Why don't you go into the lounge and read a nice gardening magazine until we've finished in here? I don't know about Mandy, but you're making me nervous!'

Mandy grinned. 'It's OK. It doesn't bother me.' Her grandad worried about two things in life; his garden and his cat. It was Grandad who'd noticed something was wrong with Smoky's ear in the first place. He told Mandy that Smoky was always scratching it and shaking his head. Mandy had gone back to Animal Ark and asked her mum and dad what it could be.

'Ear mites,' Adam Hope had suggested. 'The bites could be infected.' He'd called in at the cottage to take a look, and left Mandy there to treat poor Smoky's condition.

'Don't look!' Gran told Grandad, as Mandy settled Smoky and gently took hold of the scruff of his neck. 'Do you need any help, Mandy?'

She shook her head. 'Smoky's a good boy, aren't you? You're not going to struggle.' Speaking soothingly, Mandy very carefully put a drop or two of lukewarm liquid into the cat's ear. 'See, it's not too horrible, is it?'

Smoky opened his mouth wide and miaowed.

'There.' She massaged a spot just below his ear.

'What's that for?' Grandad ventured forward for a closer look.

'To soften the ear wax. I have to clear it out before I put some other drops in.' She worked patiently, glad that Smoky didn't fidget. Taking a piece of cotton wool, she wiped cleanser from the ear canal.

'Oops!' Grandad stood back, as suddenly Smoky shook his head. Drops splashed on to the towel.

'Nearly done,' Mandy promised. She finished off with a cotton bud, easing it down the ear to clean out the tiny, delicate folds of skin. Then Gran handed her the bottle of medicine which Adam Hope had given them. Mandy held the dropper to the infected ear and let three or four drops fall. A quick final massage and the job was done.

'Will that do the trick?' Grandad asked.

Mandy handed Smoky over to him. 'Yes. The drops will kill the mites and cure the infection.' She'd seen it done many times at the surgery, but this was the first time she'd been trusted to do it herself. She felt pleased that it had gone well.

'Excellent!' Grandad beamed at her. 'We'll make a vet of you yet.'

'I hope so,' Mandy sighed. She longed to follow in her mum and dad's footsteps and run the surgery with them.

'Long hours, lots of stress,' Gran reminded her. She cleared the table and put on a clean cloth. 'It's not an easy job.'

But Mandy couldn't think of anything she'd rather do. She'd always loved animals. 'More than people,' her dad would joke. She spent most of her spare time lending a hand at Animal Ark with sick cats, dogs, hedgehogs; any animal that needed help. With her shoulder-length blonde hair and slight figure, Mandy could often be spotted around Welford village looking for animals in trouble.

Grandad stroked Smoky under the chin. 'You have a way with them, that's for sure. Doesn't she, Smoky?'

The young grey cat purred his agreement.

'Hardly any time off.' Gran went on putting all the minus points about being a vet. 'Look at your mum and dad. It's coming up to Christmas, and they're busier than ever.'

Now that the kitchen table was back to normal, Mandy followed her gran into the lounge and helped her to lift a big cardboard box full of Christmas decorations down from a cupboard. She peered inside at the silver baubles and coloured lights. 'It's because of the cold,' she explained. 'Animals seem to have more accidents and illnesses this time of year.'

'Just like human beings, when you come to

think about it.' Grandad put Smoky down on his favourite red cushion on the sofa and came to help. 'Coughs and colds, snuffles and sneezes.' He took a tangle of Christmas lights from the box. 'That's funny. I'm sure I put these away nice and tidy last year.'

Mandy laughed at his puzzled frown. 'Shall I untangle them for you?' She loved Christmas; putting up the decorations at Animal Ark and Lilac Cottage, making and buying presents. Smoky jumped down from the sofa and came to play. He lifted his paw to bat a light that dangled from Grandad's hand.

'Yes, please.'

So Mandy sat cross-legged on the carpet with Smoky on her lap, patiently untying the knots in the wire until the lights were straightened out, ready for use.

> '*Away in a-a manger,*
> *No-o crib for a bed,*
> *The-e little Lord Jesus*
> *La-ay down his sweet head!*'

A carol singer stood at the door.

'Dad!' Mandy recognised the voice. He sang in the church choir. 'He must be practising for a concert.'

Smoky cocked an ear, miaowed, then crept off under a chair. Gran and Grandad laughed.

> *'We three Kings of Orient are,*
> *One in a taxi, one in a car . . .'*

Gran dashed to the door to let him in before he had a chance to ruin the song any further. 'Adam, come in out of the snow!'

Mandy looked up as he stopped to take off his boots at the door. There were snowflakes in his short brown hair and melting on his beard. He was zipped up inside his winter jacket, blowing warm air into his cold hands. 'Did you like my singing?' he said with a grin.

'Fantastic, Dad!'

'What's Smoky doing under there?' He unzipped his jacket and took it off.

'Hiding from the carol singer.'

'Hmm. He's got no ear for music, that cat.' Mandy's dad settled in a chair by the fire. 'Talking of ears, how is it?'

'Cured, we hope.' Mandy handed the lights to her grandad. 'Smoky seems to have stopped scratching already.'

'Well done. It gave me time to pop over to Bleakfell Hall. I had to check up on Pandora for Mrs Ponsonby. She's got a bit of a chill, that's all.

Poor Mrs P. was worried stiff.'

'*Poor Pandora*, you mean!' Gran didn't always see eye to eye with fussy Mrs Ponsonby. 'That little Pekinese gets carried everywhere. She has no chance to run around and play like any normal dog.' She brought piping-hot tea and chocolate cake through from the kitchen. 'By the way, Adam, did you mention Father Christmas to Mrs Ponsonby?'

Mandy pricked up her ears.

He clicked his fingers. 'No, sorry. I completely forgot.'

'Brain like a sieve.' Gran tapped the top of his head. 'We need to know if she has room for Rudolph at the Hall.'

'What's this?' Mandy was full of curiosity.

Gran's eyes twinkled. 'Rudolph the red-nosed reindeer. You know the tune?'

'Da-dum, de da-da da-dum . . .' Mandy's dad came in with a deep bass version.

'Don't encourage him,' Mandy sighed. 'Yes, so what about Rudolph and Bleakfell Hall?'

'Father Christmas is going to bring his reindeer to Welford for Christmas Eve!' Gran announced. 'Of course, Rudolph will be a very tired reindeer, coming all the way from Reindeerland. So he'll need a place to stay . . .'

'Oh, Gran!' Mandy sighed. She knew better

than to believe all this stuff. 'Everyone knows there's no such . . .'

'Hush. You wash your mouth out with soap and water, Mandy Hope! Father Christmas and his sleigh will be here in person, complete with reindeer. And if you don't believe me, ask your grandad!'

Mandy looked from one smiling face to another. 'Grandad? . . . Dad?'

They nodded back.

'What's going on?' The grown-ups were up to something. Mandy reached down to pick up Smoky, who'd come creeping close to the warm log fire. She cuddled him to her.

'Father Christmas will make a special guest appearance in the village square this year,' was all Grandad would say. 'Everyone's going to be there. Why don't you bring James along and find out?'

James Hunter, Mandy's best friend, lived on the edge of Welford. 'Will there really be a reindeer?'

'Two!' Gran said.

Mandy considered it. 'Maybe we will come and have a look.' Real reindeer with antlers, trotting through the snow! 'Wait a minute, I didn't think there were any reindeer left in this country. Didn't they all die out ages ago?'

'Aha!' Grandad winked. 'But there are plenty in Reindeerland!'

'Anyway,' Adam Hope said, 'that's where you're wrong. We do have reindeer in Britain. In Scotland, as a matter of fact. They belong to well-managed, domesticated herds in the Cairngorm Mountains. There! *Rangifer tarandus*, to give them their Latin name. They're supervised by the Reindeer Council, and looked after by a Mr Donald McNab.'

'Ask me anything you want to know about reindeer!' Grandad boasted. 'For instance, why do reindeer have cloven hooves?'

'I don't know; why *do* reindeer have cloven hooves?' Mandy joined in the fun. It really did seem as if Rudolph was coming for Christmas!

'To help them walk on frozen snow.' Grandad rushed on. 'And did you know, a reindeer can pull a sledge carrying three hundred pounds for a hundred miles a day?'

She shook her head. What was going on? How come they all knew so much about reindeer all of a sudden?

'Stop teasing,' Gran said at last, 'and tell poor Mandy why we're all reindeer-mad.'

'It's all in a good cause,' Grandad explained. 'This special guest appearance in the village is in aid of a little girl who lives at Beechtrees. That's the bungalow next to the main road. She and her family came to live in Welford earlier this year.

Jeremy Hastings is the new groundsman at the tennis club. Their daughter, Alex, is only five, but they've recently found out that she's seriously ill.'

Mandy tried to connect the reindeer's visit with Alex Hastings. She'd seen the girl from a distance; a tiny, red-haired child, with a bigger brother. Their hair was the first thing you noticed about them both. It was curly and shone reddish-gold in the sun. 'What's wrong with her?'

'Something to do with her heart. She needs an operation, Mandy dear.' Gran spoke softly, seriously. 'There's only one place in the world where she can get this kind of operation, and that's in America. But the Hastingses can't afford to take her there. Your grandad got to hear about it one day at the tennis club. A few people put their heads together and came up with various ways of raising money so the family could go to the States.'

'Fund-raising,' Mandy's dad chipped in. 'Everyone has been having bright ideas. Your grandad came up with this special invitation to Father Christmas and his reindeer. We hope the whole of Welford will come along, sing a few carols and put lots of money in a collection-box.'

'People have been very good so far,' Grandad said. 'We've already raised enough money for the operation, but we need another eight hundred pounds for the air fares to send Alex and her family for treatment. And we need it quickly. She must go early in the New Year for the operation, otherwise it'll be too late.'

'You mean, if she doesn't get it, she'll die?' Mandy whispered.

'I'm afraid so, love.'

For a while, everyone was silent. The logs crackled in the hearth, Smoky rubbed his soft face against Mandy's cheek.

'But if she goes to America and has the operation, the doctors think she will be completely cured,' Gran said. 'So you see, Father Christmas's visit is going to be extra-important this year.'

Slowly Mandy said, 'Does Alex know about going to America?'

Gran shook her head. 'Her mum and dad think it's best to keep quiet until they're sure they can take her. She doesn't really know how ill she is. And she certainly doesn't have a clue about Father Christmas's visit!'

Adam Hope finished his cup of tea and brushed cake crumbs from his sweater. Smoky jumped from Mandy's arms and went to see whether the crumbs were worth eating. 'I saw Alex's dad today, as a matter of fact.'

'At Animal Ark?' Mandy found the little girl's story sad but fascinating.

'Yes. He brought a kitten in for her vaccinations. They've only just got her. Alex loves animals, apparently. Her dad says the walls of her bedroom are plastered with pictures of them!' He glanced at Mandy with a little smile.

'Just like someone else we know!' Grandad teased. Mandy's own room was a portrait gallery of pets, wild animals and endangered species.

'Beechtrees is just past Susan Collins's house, isn't it?' Mandy ignored them and got to thinking ahead instead.

'That's right. Why?' Her grandad bent to plug in the Christmas lights. They lit up, a brilliant chain of blue, green and pink. 'Hey presto!'

'Oh, nothing . . .' A five-year-old girl with a new kitten! 'What's the kitten like?' she asked her dad, as casually as possible.

'She's a little brown and black tortoiseshell.'

'Sweet!' Mandy stared wistfully at Smoky, now a fully-grown cat. 'How old?'

'Four or five months, just at the playful stage. You know, she chases everything, including her own tail.'

'Aah!'

'And she has the most amazing eyes,' her dad continued. 'Big and shiny in her cute little dark face.'

'What colour?' She wanted to picture the kitten perfectly.

'Her eyes? They're a sort of bright gold colour. Traffic-light orange. Yes, that's it!' Mr Hope smiled as he stood up, ready to take Mandy home. He stroked Smoky. 'Not as good-looking as you, of course,' he said with a grin. 'But the Hastings' kitten does have the most amazing amber eyes. And that's what they've called her. Alex chose the name herself; Amber.'

They put on their jackets and boots, said goodbye to Mandy's grandparents and Smoky, and began to tramp through the snow up the lane to Animal Ark, Mr Hope whistling as they walked.

'Dad?'

'What?' He stopped mid-tune.

'I wonder if I should go and visit Alex and Amber,' Mandy said dreamily. There was a white wonderland of snow-laden trees, drifts almost a metre deep against the walls, stars in a moonlit sky.

'I don't see why not.'

'And, Dad . . .'

'Uh-oh!' He gathered snow from the wall-top and patted it into shape. His eyes gleamed as he aimed the ball at Mandy. 'Come on, this is a challenge!'

'No, Dad, I want to ask you something!' But

she couldn't resist scooping up snow and making her own snowball.

'So I gather. Am I going to say yes? I know you when you give me that look!' He was laughing now, as the first snowball flew towards him. He dodged just in time.

'Listen!' Mandy dived for more ammunition. 'You know Gran thought that the two reindeer might be able to stay at Bleakfell Hall?'

It was her dad's turn to fling a snowball. It thudded against Mandy's shoulder. 'Direct hit! Yes, Mrs Ponsonby has an empty stable at the back of the Hall.'

'Well, we could look after them at Animal Ark instead, couldn't we? We've got room in the residential unit. I mean, reindeer aren't all that big!' She stood with her arm raised, fresh snow poised ready.

'Gi-normous!' Mr Hope dodged and slipped. He landed flat on his back.

Mandy ran over and stood, hands on hips, 'But Mrs Ponsonby wouldn't have a clue how to look after them. We would! You and mum must know all about reindeer.'

'Flattery will get you . . . everywhere!' He grinned back up at her.

'You mean yes? The reindeer can stay with us?' She hauled him to his feet.

'For a couple of nights. As long as your mum agrees.'

'Yippee!' Mandy charged into a drift and kicked up loose snow. It sprayed up and sparkled. 'Oh, Dad, thanks! Oh, brilliant!' She ran ahead up the lane to Animal Ark. Real reindeer were coming to stay!

2

'Two reindeer?' Emily Hope was talking on the phone in Reception. Jean Knox, Animal Ark's receptionist, stood listening, her glasses perched high on her forehead. Simon, their nurse, came through from a treatment room, ready for morning surgery. He raised his eyebrows at Mandy when he overheard the conversation.

It was early the next morning; only three days to go until Christmas Eve, and Mandy was keeping her fingers firmly crossed. Her mum had just rung the owner of the reindeer herd in Scotland to make arrangements for the visit.

'Rudolph and Dasher?' Mrs Hope smiled. 'And

you'll bring their food with them?'

Mandy's eyes shone. 'We're having two reindeer to stay this Christmas!' she whispered to Simon.

'You must be joking!' Glancing up from the appointment book, he realised that Mandy was serious. 'When?'

'Tomorrow, Wednesday.'

'How will they travel? By flying across the rooftops?' Simon winked at Jean, who seemed to think that the entire Hope family had finally gone crazy.

'I don't know yet. Hang on a minute.' Mandy listened in again.

'We have an open-air compound at the back of Animal Ark, where we exercise the patients. It's small, but secure. I think that should be all right. You say the reindeer need to stay out overnight . . . Yes, OK. Someone could meet you in Walton and show you the road over the moor to Welford. It's hard to find if you don't know your way around . . . We've had snow, but the main roads are fairly clear. Yes, fine.'

They waited as arrangements went ahead.

'Tomorrow afternoon? Yes, one of us will be there. We'll meet you outside the bus station in town . . . you should be able to park a trailer there . . . Just look out for our Animal Ark Land-rover . . . yes, bye, Mr McNab!' Emily Hope nodded as she put down the phone.

'Correct me if I'm wrong, but did I just hear you break your strictest Animal Ark rule?' Jean asked in disbelief. She'd known the Hopes a long time, and never in living memory had Mandy's mum and dad agreed to let an animal who didn't need treatment come to stay.

'You did.' Mrs Hope put on her white coat.

'Here comes our first patient.' Mandy hopped off her stool and went to the window. She wanted to change the subject. A car struggled down the lane through the snow. It looked like the Parker Smythes' big four-wheel drive.

'Well, I never!' Jean still couldn't believe it.

'They're coming down from a place near Aviemore,' Mrs Hope said. 'It's quite a journey. Donald McNab is driving down in a trailer . . . to help Father Christmas deliver presents in Welford!'

'Mum!' It looked as if Mandy would have to go along with the Father Christmas thing, though she considered herself much too old.

'What's wrong? You still hang up your stocking for him, don't you?'

'Yes, but . . . oh, OK, you win!' Mandy beamed.

'It's all in a good cause.' Her mum explained to Jean the idea behind the reindeers' visit. 'We're trying to raise money to send little Alex Hastings to America. You know about her operation, don't you?' Soon everyone in Welford would be in on it, thought Mandy.

'Good idea. I'll be there,' Jean promised. 'After all, it is Christmas.'

'Seven-thirty in the square on Christmas Eve?' Simon asked. 'Count me in too.' Mrs Parker Smythe and her eight-year-old daughter, Imogen, had just brought their pet rabbits, Button and Barney, into the surgery. He showed them into a treatment room. 'Did you hear about Father Christmas's special visit?' he asked them, as the door swung to.

'The more the merrier,' Emily Hope smiled. She turned to Mandy. 'Happy now?'

'I can't wait!'

'Well, why not go and visit Alex, like you planned? I'm sure she could do with some company.'

'Now?' Mandy would normally help out in the surgery during the school holidays.

'Why not? We won't be busy here, not in this weather. And you could tell her there's a special treat in store this Christmas.'

'But not exactly what the treat is?' Mandy scrambled out of her white coat and grabbed her jacket.

Mrs Hope put her head to one side, ready to start work. 'No,' she said. 'Let's keep Father

Christmas as a nice surprise!'

'Alex likes animals,' Mandy promised James. She'd called at the Hunter's house, and James had decided to bring his dog, Blackie, along to Beechtrees.

The black Labrador padded through the snow ahead of them, leaving a narrow trail of footprints. When he came to the wide gates of Susan Collins's grand house, he stopped.

'No, Blackie, that's not where we're going today.' James ordered him on. James was dressed for the snow in a padded jacket and a baseball cap worn back-to-front. The wind had reddened his cheeks, and his glasses reflected the bright light as he and Mandy loped along after Blackie.

Beechtrees was tucked away under the shadow of some tall trees a few hundred metres along the main road from Susan's house. Today there were few cars on the road; only a yellow snow-remover trundling towards them, with Jeremy Hastings sitting at the controls. The plough had been clearing a track from the tennis club towards the main road after the snowfall of the previous night.

'Hello there.' Mr Hastings drew near, then leaned sideways. He was puzzled by the sight of Blackie, James and Mandy knee-deep in the fresh snow.

'Hello.' Mandy knew him as friendly in a quiet sort of way, never excited or annoyed. She and

James had seen him at work around the tennis courts that autumn.

Blackie spoiled the introductions by barking at the snow-plough.

'Sorry.' James blushed and told him to sit. 'He's never seen one close up before.'

'That's OK.' Jeremy Hastings decided to take a break. He climbed down from the cab. 'I know you two, don't I?'

'Yes. I'm James Hunter, and this is Blackie.'

'And I'm Mandy Hope.' Somehow, because Mr Hastings was shy, Mandy was self-conscious too. She felt her face grow hot behind her woollen scarf and hat.

'The vets' daughter?'

She nodded.

'I took Alex's kitten up to Animal Ark for her yesterday. Nice place.' He didn't waste words. 'Alex doesn't get out much at the moment.'

'No. That's why we've brought Blackie to see her,' James said.

Mandy's blonde hair fell around her face as she took off her hat. 'We heard she likes animals.'

'She's mad about them!' For the first time, Jeremy Hastings smiled. 'Completely cuckoo. She'll love you, Blackie. Why don't you all come in?'

Mandy felt that the ice was broken. She grinned

at James and followed the groundsman between two tall beech trees, up a path towards the bungalow.

'Alex!' Mr Hastings opened the door and knocked snow off his boots. 'You've got visitors!'

They waited for an answer, but none came.

'She's a bit shy with strangers,' her father told them. 'Hang on a sec.' He kicked off his wellingtons and went inside.

'Sit, Blackie.' James made him wait inside the porch. He and Mandy stared curiously into the hallway.

'What do you want?' a voice challenged from behind them.

They spun round. Blackie jumped up. There in the front garden, peering from behind a bush, was a small boy with bright ginger hair. His eyes were greeny-grey, his face covered in freckles. He wore a navy-blue fleece jacket zipped to his chin, and an expression that said 'Get lost!'

'We've come to play with Alex,' Mandy answered carefully. The boy looked about seven years old.

'Oh, her.' He turned away in disgust. 'She doesn't want to play.' He trudged back on to the lawn and kicked at the deep snow. 'I'm her brother, and she won't even play with me.'

Mandy couldn't tell who the boy was most

angry with, but his tone of voice and his deep frown made her guess that it was everyone and everything. He was what Gran would call 'mardy'. This meant he sulked a lot.

'I'll play with you,' James volunteered. It was chilly standing on the porch waiting for Alex to appear. 'We could build a snowman.'

'Where?'

'There on the lawn.'

'How tall?'

'As tall as you like.'

'Up to the roof of the bungalow?' The boy looked up at the single storey house.

'Well, maybe not that tall.' James went ahead anyway. He jumped from the step into the garden and began to scoop snow into a rough pile. 'Let's see how fat we can make him.'

Mandy pulled her hat from her pocket. 'He can wear this when you've finished him.'

Slowly the boy came and took it. 'Can he wear your scarf too?'

'OK.' She unwound it and handed it over.

Satisfied, he ran back to James. Soon they were both hard at work on the snowman's body.

'There, what did I tell you?' Mr Hastings returned at last, holding his daughter's hand. 'Here's a dog come all this way in the snow to see you. He's called Blackie.'

Blackie stood up and wagged his tail at the sound of his name.

Mandy knelt and put an arm around his neck. 'He won't bite,' she said softly. 'He's a nice doggie.'

Alex Hastings let go of her father's hand and took a halting step forward. She was small for a five-year-old; pale and thin, wearing a dark blue corduroy dress. Her curly hair was even brighter than Mandy's mum's; the reddest hair that she had ever seen.

Alex's big green eyes grew wide as she reached out a tiny hand to stroke Blackie. 'He's all wet!' She took it quickly away.

'That's melted snow. Blackie likes the snow. He tries to eat it!'

Alex stroked him again. 'His ears are nice and soft.'

'He's one big softie really.' Mandy smiled as the little girl grew bolder. 'Would your new kitten like to meet him?'

Alex looked up at her dad. 'Won't the dog chase Amber?'

'I don't think so. Blackie's probably used to cats. Why not fetch Amber from your bedroom and see?'

As Alex went slowly through one of the doors leading off from the square hallway, Mr Hastings smiled at Mandy. 'Bring Blackie inside and let me close the door. Alex's mum is fixing hot chocolate for everyone. We can all do with it on a day like today.'

Mandy smiled back, stepped in and looked round at the cream coloured walls, the big mirror and framed family photographs.

'Dad, Amber won't come!' Alex called in a high, panicky voice. 'She's hiding under the bed.'

There was a faint miaow. Blackie pricked up his ears and whined.

'No, she's not! She's running away!'

They heard rapid little feet pattering and jumping from surface to surface, then a small black and brown shape hurtled through the door. The kitten somersaulted into the hall.

'Oh, Amber!' Alex cried from her bedroom.

'It's OK, here she is!' Mr Hastings cornered the kitten and picked her up.

Mandy held on to Blackie as Alex came slowly over and took Amber from her father. All Mandy could see was a bundle of wriggling fur, a long, fluffy tail and a little pair of pointed ears. 'She's gorgeous!' she exclaimed.

'Amber, be good,' Alex scolded. 'Say hello to Blackie.'

But the kitten caught sight of the big black dog and stared. Her golden eyes flashed, and she opened her mouth wide and hissed.

'No, you have to be nice to him,' Alex insisted. She brought her up closer. 'Nice doggie. See, Amber; nice, nice doggie!'

Good-natured Blackie sniffed at the kitten. Amber's ears and whiskers twitched. She put out a paw to pat the dog's black nose.

'See, you like him!' Soon it was safe to let go of the kitten. Alex put her on the carpet and watched the two animals stalk in circles around each other. Blackie towered over the kitten, but he was very gentle. Amber, on the other hand, thought that playing meant jumping up at Blackie and catching hold of his neck. She clung on for dear life.

Alex gasped, then laughed. 'They're having a game!'

Mandy told her all about Blackie and James. 'James is my best friend. He helps us with the animals at Animal Ark.' She explained that her mum and dad looked after sick animals.

Alex didn't take her eyes off Amber and Blackie. 'Are they all sick?' she asked slowly.

'Who, the patients who come to my house?' Mandy nodded. 'But most of them get better. It's like a hospital for animals.'

The little girl turned to her with a serious face. 'I've been to hospital.'

'I know,' Mandy said gently.

'I might have to go again, so they can make me better. Then I can play out with William.'

'That's her brother,' Mr Hastings explained.

'I know. We met him in the garden. James is out there building a snowman with him.' Mandy took Alex to the glass door to look outside. The snowman was already as high as William's shoulder.

'Who's building a snowman?' Alex's mother popped her head around the kitchen door.

'William and James.' Alex peered out wistfully at the snowy scene. Then she turned her attention back to the two animals. 'Amber's got a friend,' she told her mum.

Mrs Hastings stepped into view. She was small

and neat, in dark trousers and a soft, fawn-coloured jumper. Her short hair was a darker red than her children's, with rich coppery tints.

She smiled at Mandy. 'So have you,' she said to her daughter. 'A new friend. What a lovely surprise!'

Mandy was soon made to feel welcome in the Hastings' house. Alex took her and Blackie into her bedroom. From there they could see James and William out in the garden. The snowman was growing; he had a head and a face made from twigs and stones.

'What's Father Christmas bringing you?' Alex sat on her bed with Amber on her lap. Surrounded by pillows and cushions, she looked like a little red-haired doll.

'I'm not sure.' Mandy smiled.

'Do you believe in him?' Alex asked solemnly. She didn't give Mandy a chance to reply. 'I do! I wrote to him with a list of things.'

'What did you ask for?'

'Well, it's not things exactly. Anyway, I can't tell. It's a secret. Otherwise it won't come true, like a wish.'

Beneath the bright chatter, Mandy suspected that Alex was sad. From the way she sat stroking her kitten, she could even imagine what Alex's wish might have been. 'Dear Father Christmas, Please give me an operation to make me better, so I can go out and play.'

'Do you like reindeers?' Alex chatted on. 'I do! My favourite is Rudolph. Who's your favourite?'

Mandy glanced up at the giant colour pictures of kittens and puppies, ponies and hamsters. She could hardly see a square centimetre of bare wall space. 'Rudolph.' She bit her lip. Sometimes it was difficult not to spill the beans. Little did Alex know it, but she was about to get a visit from her favourite reindeer!

'Poor Rudolph, he couldn't join in any reindeer games, could he?' Alex sighed.

'Because his nose was too red. They didn't like him,' Mandy reminded her.

'I would have let him join in anyway.'

'Me too.' Mandy sat on the floor with Blackie, happy to talk to Alex as if Rudolph was a real, live reindeer. Alex seemed to know the story inside out.

'What did it matter what colour his nose was?' Alex was determined to stick up for Santa's problem helper. 'When I'm better, anyone who wants to can play with me! I'll go back to school, and *everyone* can be my friend!'

Mandy agreed. Suddenly, there was a loud thud against the window. They turned quickly, in time to see a flattened snowball sliding down the glass.

'William!' Alex gasped. The windowpane had rattled. Startled, Amber had jumped from her lap and gone into hiding. Blackie gave a sharp bark.

'Alex, come and look!' The boy's voice from the garden was high and bossy. Another snowball landed against the glass.

Slowly Alex uncrossed her legs. Mandy helped her from the bed. She could only move at a snail's pace, Mandy realised, and was quickly out of breath.

'Come here. Look at this!'

From the window, the girls could see two snowmen. One wore Mandy's red and white striped hat and scarf. The other had James's cap perched on his head.

'What's going on in here?' Mrs Hastings came rushing into the room with a worried frown. She glanced at the melting snowballs sliding slowly down the windowpane. 'What was that noise?'

'William's snowballs. Look what they've built in the garden!' Alex's face was bright with admiration.

But Mrs Hastings was annoyed as she came to the window.

From outside, William saw his mother and yelled. 'Mum, look!' He sounded faint through the glass, but they could tell he was proud of the snowmen. 'Can Alex come out and see?'

Mrs Hastings tapped hard on the window. 'No, she can't!' she mouthed. 'And you come inside at once!'

Mandy saw the smile vanish from William's face. James stood by, unsure.

'Alex, it's time for your medicine,' her mother said sharply. Frowning, she left the room to fetch it.

'William's for it now,' Alex whispered. 'He's not supposed to do things that make me jump.' She sighed and retreated to her bed. 'Now he'll think it's my fault that he's in trouble again.'

'Oh, I'm sure he won't,' Mandy began. But she heard doors bang and Mrs Hastings's voice going on at her son.

'. . . No consideration . . . making loud noises . . . you're seven years old; old enough to know better, William!'

Alex hung her head and put her hands over her ears.

'We'd better be off,' Mandy said quickly. James still stood out there in the cold.

Alex nodded. 'I have to have a nap after my medicine anyway.' She blushed and smiled. 'Thanks for bringing Blackie to see me.'

'Thanks for showing me Amber.' The kitten peeped out from under the bed, her eyes shining big and golden. 'Enjoy the snowmen!' Alex would be able to see them from her bed. Mandy smiled again and left.

Outside, she found James waiting for her, and, at the gate, the worried figure of Jeremy Hastings.

'Alex has to be kept nice and quiet, see,' he said to explain Mrs Hastings's anger about the snowballs. 'No exertion. It's doctors' orders. Of course, if she gets her operation, it'll be a different story. She'll be running round just like she was before.'

'Grandad says the fund-raising is going really well,' Mandy said.

He nodded and smiled grimly. 'A lot depends on this Father Christmas thing.'

'Don't worry. It'll be amazing; a sleigh, real reindeer – Alex will love it!'

'You didn't mention it to her?'

'No.' It had been hard, but Mandy had kept the secret.

'Good. It's bound to cheer her up, isn't it?' Mr Hastings gazed up at the trees, as if he would find an answer there to his family's problems. 'Alex has always loved Father Christmas and his reindeer.'

Mandy and James said goodbye. They left Mr Hastings standing by his snow-plough, gazing up at the grey sky.

3

'I'm sorry I'm late.' Donald McNab strolled up to the Animal Ark Land-rover.

It was just before tea next day, and Mandy and James had driven into Walton with Mr Hope to meet their special guests. After an hour of sitting freezing in the car, with James snuffling and sneezing into his hankie, Mandy's dad had nipped off to buy warm drinks. It had been a long, cold wait.

'Aye, I lost my way,' the Scotsman explained in a heavy accent. He sounded very calm. 'Took a couple of wrong turnings in York. Terrible place to drive through. I went around the old city walls three times before I found the right exit. My head was spinning by the time I got out.'

'That's OK.' Mandy and James looked eagerly for the reindeer in Mr McNab's trailer, which he'd parked a few metres up the road. They weren't interested in why he was late.

'I thought maybe I'd missed you.' He shook hands as first James, then Mandy jumped down on to the pavement. His grey eyes shone with good humour, his handshake was firm. 'It was good of you to wait.'

'Dad won't be long,' Mandy said. 'Mr McNab, can we go and take a peep?' All day she'd been looking forward to this.

'At Rudolph and Dasher? Aye, go right ahead. And call me Don!' He fished deep in the pocket of his weatherproof jacket. 'Here, you can give them a wee treat for being cooped up in that trailer for so long.'

They took a handful each of what looked suspiciously like scraps of chewed leather. James sniffed them and wrinkled his nose.

'Dried mushrooms,' Don laughed. 'They love 'em!'

Mandy couldn't wait a moment longer. She ran ahead. From inside the grey trailer came a loud shuffling and knocking of hooves. She saw that the back doors were half open, like stable doors, and as she drew near, two heads loomed out; two long noses, two pairs of dark brown eyes, and two sets of enormous antlers.

Mandy held her breath. The animals were only the height of a small Welsh pony, but their antlers were huge, branching off like mighty boughs on a tree. They curved over the reindeer's heads as they nodded and poked them out of the trailer.

'Go ahead!' Don encouraged. 'They won't harm you!'

Gingerly Mandy reached up with the mushrooms. The nearest reindeer bent to nibble at them with his velvety mouth.

'That's Dasher.'

James followed suit, letting the other reindeer nip food from his palm.

'And that's Rudolph. Say hello, boys!'

The reindeer snorted and grunted. The trailer shook as they shifted their weight.

By now a small crowd had gathered. Walton had never seen a reindeer in the flesh. Word went round for people to come and look at their magnificent antlers. Mothers came with children, shopkeepers stood out on the pavement. One bus-driver even stopped his bus to let his passengers see, while Don McNab fielded eager questions.

'They've come to help Father Christmas,' he explained to the smallest children. 'They have to pull his sleigh through the snow.'

'When?'

'Where?'

'Will we see them?' More questions, more round eyes and open mouths.

'Aye, you will if you come to Welford on Christmas Eve,' Don told them. 'That's when the old gentleman will bring your presents!' He winked at James and Mandy.

Through all the fuss, Rudolph and Dasher chewed contentedly, until Adam Hope came back with the drinks and the children had to say goodbye.

'Do you think you'll be able to follow us OK?' Mandy's dad asked Don, after the two men had met.

But Mandy came up with a better idea. She arranged to drive with Don in the reindeer van. 'Just in case they can't keep up,' she explained.

'Och aye, I don't want to get lost again!' Don helped her into the passenger seat. All the way home, out of town and across the moor, Mandy was able to fire questions at him.

'What do reindeer eat?' she asked, hoping she'd be able to help feed them later.

'Grass, moss, ferns, bark, oh aye and mushrooms, of course,' Don answered, as he drove carefully down the hill towards Welford. The whole valley lay under a blanket of snow, and the village lights twinkled in the dusk. He stifled a yawn. 'I'm away to my bed early tonight.'

Mandy smiled happily. 'We'll take care of the reindeer for you,' she promised.

'Aye, I know you will. Anyhow, I've a busy day tomorrow.'

It would be Thursday tomorrow, the day before

Christmas Eve. 'Where do you have to go?' Mandy asked.

'I've to drive the reindeer to a children's hospital in Leeds tomorrow morning. The old gentleman will be handing out presents there.'

Mandy shot a puzzled look at the cheerful little Scotsman. He had short grey hair, a square face, a nice, outdoorsy feel. 'This old gentleman . . .' she began.

'Father Christmas, aye?'

'I mean, aren't you . . . Isn't it really? . . .' She stammered to a halt. Here was another grown-up who liked to tease.

'Me?' He roared with laughter and thumped the steering wheel. 'Oh no, dearie! Don't ever let him catch you saying such a thing, or there'll be no presents for you this year!'

He went on chuckling as they followed Mr Hope and James through the village, past the pub and the post office, along the lane to Animal Ark.

4

'Hold him steady,' Don told Mandy as she led Rudolph down the ramp from the trailer into the yard.

The reindeer tossed his head and pawed the ground stiffly until he grew used to his new surroundings.

'Here come the guests of honour.' Emily Hope stood on the step after evening surgery.

'They're . . . awesome!' Simon gave a low whistle. 'Look at those antlers!'

Rudolph grunted suspiciously, then allowed Mandy to lead him on. She took him round the back to the residential area and gave him a reward.

'Good boy.' She stroked his thick white winter mane.

'Steady as you go.' Don steered James and Dasher down the ramp. He took a look at the high wire fence surrounding the exercise compound. 'Aye, this'll do nicely.'

Mandy breathed a sigh of relief. The reindeer's long journey had ended safely. 'Will they need food?' she asked Don, anxious again as Rudolph and Dasher began to paw at the snow. 'They must be hungry.'

'No need. They can dig, see.'

The reindeer lowered their heads and began to scrape with their antlers, using them as giant snow-shovels. Soon they were down to green grass and grazing happily.

Mandy, James, Adam and Emily Hope, Simon and Jean all gathered round to watch. 'They don't seem to mind an audience,' Mr Hope said quietly.

'Och, they're used to it. They're at the centre of the action wherever they go.' Don went to fetch his own bag from the battered white van. He looked up at the soft snowflakes floating out of the dark sky. 'Good reindeer weather. It reminds them of home.'

'Come inside and get warm.' Unless there was an emergency call during the evening, Emily Hope had finished work for the day. She took

Don's bag and carried it into the house. Simon and Jean went inside to tidy up the surgery.

'Aye, in a wee while.' Don grinned at Mandy and James. 'I just want to show these two the sleigh belonging to the old gentleman himself!' He stayed out in the yard as the other grown-ups went indoors.

James and Mandy shrugged and followed.

'But it's the trailer!' James was disappointed. Father Christmas's sleigh was just like any other trailer that you would see on a farm, or at a horse show.

'Not just any ordinary trailer, young Jim!' Don McNab leaped into action. He unscrewed nuts and bolts, removed the detachable roof, folded down fibreglass flaps, and soon transformed the trailer into what looked for all the world like an old-fashioned sleigh.

'Wow!' James was impressed. The painted side panels hid the wheels and looked like imitation sledge runners.

'Abracadabra! We hitch the reindeer on to the front, and jingle bells, off we go!'

'That's really neat,' Mandy said.

'Aye, it is.'

'Who thought of it?' James tipped his glasses more firmly on to his nose and went to inspect it more closely.

'I did.' Don was proud of his handiwork. 'I use it to tour the country at Christmas time. In two shakes I can turn the trailer into the old gentleman's sleigh. He arrives in style to visit the kiddies in hospital, or turn on the Christmas lights, whatever they want.'

'I like it!' James examined the hinges and moulded fibreglass, and the metal shafts which harnessed the reindeer.

'Then why not come with us tomorrow?' Don promptly invited them both along. 'We're off to visit the wee kids in hospital in Leeds. You two can keep me on the right road.' He reminded them how hopeless he was at finding his way.

'Great; we could help look after Rudolph and Dasher!' Mandy jumped at the chance. She ran inside to ask her mum and dad.

'Yes, fine,' Emily Hope said. She stood by the stove in the warm kitchen. 'Would you tell Don that supper's ready?'

They sat down to steaming plates of thick soup and piles of fresh bread. Don McNab ate with a ravenous appetite, entertaining them with stories of the reindeer herd at home. Mandy lapped it all up; the rolling sound of the Scotsman's voice, the picture he painted of snowy mountains and magnificent animals.

Before she went to bed, Mandy went outside

to check one last time on Rudolph and Dasher. They were still happily shovelling snow with their antlers to reach the grass. Tomorrow, Mandy and James would go with them to visit the children in hospital. The day after would be Grandad's fund-raising event for Alex. Mandy sighed and let the light snowflakes settle on her nose. This was going to be the most exciting Christmas ever!

'Two days to go before I open my stocking!' Simon rubbed his hands as he came in next morning. He was wearing layers of jumpers under his jacket, and a woolly hat was pulled down over his forehead. Outside, it was sunny but freezing cold.

Mandy had been up bright and early, along with her parents, while their Scots guest slept in. She'd already answered the phone to half a dozen worried pet owners. The appointment book was full.

'Just think, back home for Christmas Day; a lie-in, presents, turkey and Christmas pud!' Simon put on his white coat.

'Can we fit Mr Pickard in?' Mandy ran her finger down the list of appointments. Walter was on the phone to say that his old cat, Tom, was off-colour.

Simon nodded. 'We'll squeeze him in, but don't tell Jean.'

So Mandy made the appointment. 'He'd like to come in straight away. He sounds worried.'

And that was the start of a pre-Christmas rush at Animal Ark. At half-past eight, Jean arrived and took over from Mandy at the desk. Mandy put on her white coat, ready to help her mum and dad. There were three dogs, two cats, a hamster and a hedgehog to feed and clean.

And of course, there were Rudolph and Dasher to see to. As she went out with a special mix of oats and molasses recommended by Don, the reindeer raised their heads in greeting. Dasher trotted straight up to his dish of cereal and tucked in, but Rudolph took one sniff at his and turned up his nose. *That's strange*, Mandy thought. She patted his shaggy neck, frowned and went back inside.

Then there was a waiting-room full of patients, with old Walter Pickard and Tom at the front of the queue. Mandy was on hand as they came into Mr Hope's treatment room.

'Let's take a look at this old chap.' Mandy's dad waited for Walter to lift Tom out of his basket.

Tom appeared, sad and bedraggled. Normally a sturdy, heavyweight cat, black and white, barrel-shaped, with a black patch of fur over one eye, today he looked thin and ill. He snuffled, his head hung low, his eyes dull.

Adam Hope examined his eyes and throat. 'Has he been eating properly?'

Walter shook his head. 'He's gone right off his grub. It's not like Tom.'

'Has he been sneezing? Coughing?' Mr Hope beckoned Mandy to take a look. 'See these little ulcers on his tongue?'

She nodded. 'Is it cat flu?'

'It looks like it.' He took Tom's temperature and confirmed that it was high.

Walter sighed. The old man treated Tom as a companion. Like him, the cat was a tough customer, but getting on in years. And this year, Walter had forgotten to have him vaccinated. 'Can you do anything for him?'

Mr Hope stroked Tom. 'He'll need antibiotics to treat any secondary infection, and plenty of fluid, but you should be able to take him home and nurse him there. You'll have to keep him warm. Clean up his eyes and nostrils if they get blocked. Poor old chap, he's having trouble breathing.'

'He's feeling sorry for himself all right.'

Mr Hope decided to dose Tom with antibiotics there and then. Mandy helped to hold the cat, as her father showed Walter the best way to get the syrup down his throat. 'Remember, this is a virus infection,' he explained. 'You'll have to wash Tom's bedding and feeding bowls, then disinfect them. Don't let him near other cats, OK?'

Walter promised to take good care of him. 'Thank you, Mr Hope,' he said meekly, as he put Tom back in his basket.

'Give us a ring to let us know how you're getting along with the medicine. And don't worry, we'll soon have him back on his feet, terrorising the neighbourhood again!'

The old man smiled weakly. 'I hope you're right.' He shuffled out of the room with his pet.

Mr Hope glanced at Mandy. 'And don't you worry! Tom will be fine.'

'It's not that.' Mandy frowned. 'It's Rudolph.' She remembered that he too had sounded chesty when she took out the dish of food. And he had the look that Tom had come in with; dull-eyed and moping. She told her dad how the reindeer had turned down the oats.

'Hmm. Do you want me to take a look?'

Though the waiting-room was full to overflowing, Mandy nodded.

'Come on then, quick!'

They went out together into the snowy compound, where the difference between the two reindeer was now quite clear. Dasher, whom Mandy recognised by his shorter antlers and dark coat, came trotting nimbly, hooves clicking. But Rudolph kept his distance and gazed listlessly. When Mandy and Adam Hope approached him,

he simply lowered his head and sat down in the snow.

'Not so good.' Adam Hope frowned. 'It looks like you were right, Mandy. We may have a sick reindeer on our hands.'

They examined Rudolph and brought Don out to look. Mr Hope diagnosed a viral infection which needed the kind of treatment he'd prescribed for Tom. 'Plenty of food, plenty of water. Keep him separate from Dasher.'

Don nodded. He had talked Rudolph back on to his feet and stood patting his neck.

'He should be over it in a day or two. Perhaps even in time for Christmas. It's a kind of twenty-four hour reindeer flu.'

But this left Don with a problem. 'I can't let the kiddies down this morning,' he told them.

'Can Dasher pull the sleigh by himself?' Mandy asked.

'He can just about manage it if Father Christmas walks alongside instead of sitting on top. You think I should go ahead and leave Rudolph behind to recover?'

'I'll stay here to look after him!' Mandy promised.

So when James arrived, full of cold but ready for the trip into Leeds, he and Don led Dasher into the trailer and prepared to set off alone.

'You're sure you don't mind, Mandy?' James asked.

'No. We're really busy in the surgery in any case. I'll be more use staying here.'

'Aye, you look after Rudolph.' Don sat at the wheel, ready to move off.

'. . . the red-nosed reindeer!' James grinned.

'Ha-ha!' She grinned back. 'Don't get lost!' she called, as the van and trailer eased out of the yard.

'Very funny!' James leaned out and waved a map. 'Don't worry, we'll be back by teatime!'

'Mandy!' Jean called her inside. 'Would you mind manning the telephone for the next hour? Surgery is overrunning, and I did promise that I'd nip into the village to meet Lydia Fawcett for coffee. I tried to ring High Cross to cancel it, but she'd already left.'

Mandy agreed willingly. She took over in Reception, seeing the last patients into the treatment rooms and answering the busy phone. Every now and then she would glance out at Rudolph. He seemed the same; no better, no worse.

'Welford 703267, Animal Ark!' She picked up the phone. It was nearly lunchtime. Her dad had gone out on an emergency call to Sam Western's dairy herd at Upper Welford Hall. Her mum was busy treating patients in the unit.

'Hello?' A woman's voice hesitated. 'This may not be the right thing to do, but I wondered if you could give me some advice?'

'Mrs Hastings?' Mandy recognised the voice. 'Is it something to do with Amber?' Her first thought was that the kitten might have developed a case of cat flu, like Walter's Tom.

'Oh, hello, Mandy. Actually it is. It's OK, she's not ill. It's nothing like that.'

Mandy was relieved but puzzled.

'It's a silly thing in a way . . .'

'Shall I fetch Mum?'

'No, I really don't want to bother her. Perhaps you could help. You see, Amber's been rather naughty this morning. She was in a mischievous mood, playing hide-and-seek. Anyway, Alex lost her. We looked, but we couldn't find her anywhere inside the house. But when my husband came home for lunch a few minutes ago, he spotted where Amber was.' Mrs Hastings paused for breath.

'Where?' Mandy pictured the garden path, the porch, the single storey building.

'On the roof! I went out to look, and there she was, the naughty little thing, perched halfway up, refusing to come down!'

'Do you think she's stuck?'

'We don't know. Jeremy says that if she managed to get up, surely she can manage to get down. He thinks we should wait and see.'

Mandy knew that cats, even kittens of Amber's age, had excellent balance. On the other hand, it must be very cold up there on the roof. 'Have you tried to tempt her down?'

'Yes. I've just put out a saucer of milk on the front step. We've been calling her, but she takes no notice. What do you think we should do?'

'Keep trying,' Mandy decided. 'Try some food

as well as milk. And tell Alex that cats usually come down when they're ready.'

'Right.' Mrs Hastings sounded reassured. 'It's just that at the moment we don't like anything to upset her. But anyway, you're probably right. We'll try the food, Mandy. Thank you very much.'

'That's OK. Will you ring us when Amber comes down?' Mandy would be uneasy until the problem was solved. She put down the phone and checked with Simon that she'd done the right thing.

'Fine,' he confirmed. He brought a list of fresh jobs for Mandy to be getting on with. 'Can you help me put a fresh dressing on the cocker spaniel's leg? Then we have to fit an Elizabethan collar to the border collie.'

'To stop him biting his stitches?' The farm dog had a jagged wound on his back. The collar made a cone shape around the dog's head so that he couldn't turn and tug at the affected area.

Simon nodded. They went ahead with the routine tasks, then, in the middle of the afternoon, Emily Hope popped her head around the door to check in with them. 'It's all go!' She looked busy but perfectly in control. The phone rang again. 'Get that, Mandy, would you?'

Mandy dashed into Reception. Perhaps it was

Lisa Hastings with good news about Amber.
'Welford 703267.'

'Hi, Mandy, it's me!' James sounded far off.
'Listen, you'll never guess what's happened.'

'Hi, James. You got lost?'

'No. We found the hospital OK. Father Christmas did his bit, even though I didn't actually see it. The nurses said my cold made me infectious. Anyway, all the kids got their presents. Dasher went into the ward with him. They loved it.'

'So?' She leaned sideways to look out of the window for a quick check on Rudolph.

'We're snowed in.'

'What?' Her jaw dropped.

'We're stuck here in Leeds. It's snowing like crazy, the roads are blocked, and we can't move!'

'Oh no!' If they didn't get back before tomorrow, this would turn into a major crisis. 'For how long?'

'No one knows. They're out with the snowplough and gritters, but you should see it, Mandy! People are saying that it might go on all day and all night!'

'Where are you exactly?'

'We're still at the hospital. Don was able to put Dasher out on the lawn, so he's happy. But he reckons we might not get back to Welford tonight.'

'What about tomorrow?' Christmas Eve; Father Christmas's special appearance. The collection for Alex. Her operation! Mandy's heart sank.

'We don't know. We hope we can make it. Don says to keep our fingers crossed. He said to ask how Rudolph is.'

'He's OK. He still looks down in the dumps, though. Listen, James . . .'

'Quick, Mandy. My money's running out.'

The phone line crackled. 'What are we going to do if you don't make it?'

Bip-bip-bip! The line buzzed and went dead. Mandy put down the phone with an empty click. She almost panicked. What a day! One crisis after another. And now, with just twenty-four hours to go to the big event, they had no sleigh, just one sick reindeer, and no Father Christmas!

5

'Mandy, what on earth's the matter?' Her grandad strode into the surgery in his walking-boots, thick socks and a waxed jacket. He was on his way to the village, and had called in to see if they needed anything from the post office.

'Oh, Grandad; Father Christmas – Don McNab – is snowed in. He might not be able to get back for tomorrow night!'

'Well, I never!' Even Tom Hope was put off his stride. 'But we've already told everyone to come. They're even travelling over from Walton to see him. They're expecting us to put on a good show.' He sat for a moment on a chair in the waiting-room. He took off his thick gloves and ran a hand through his grey hair. 'And we're relying on that collection money to raise the final eight hundred pounds.'

'I know.' Mandy began to think. She stopped panicking, determined not to look on the black side. 'If the worst comes to the worst, at least we'll still have Rudolph.'

'But no sleigh and no Father Christmas,' Grandad groaned.

'No, and I suppose we don't even know if Rudolph will be better in time.' Mandy's nerve faltered as she glanced outside. It was the darkest time of the year. The light was already fading from an overcast sky. But at least it wasn't snowing here in Welford, and Rudolph was starting to scrape away at the snow to find the greenest grass shoots. 'But let's say he does make it,' she went on. 'Dad said it might be a twenty-four hour thing.'

'Yes?' Grandad looked weary. 'All that planning, and it could come to nothing,' he mumbled.

'Listen!' Mandy went and crouched beside him, willing him not to give in. 'Rudolph looks OK; at least we'll have one reindeer!'

'And one is better than none?'

'Yes, and maybe the sleigh isn't that important. Or maybe someone like Mr Western or Mr

Collins could lend us a trailer. We could decorate it with Christmas lights to make it look a bit like a sleigh!'

'A do-it-yourself effort?' Grandad picked up.

'Yes!' There was no stopping Mandy now. 'Ernie Bell's good at making things. Maybe we could get him to help. And it would be easy to get a stand-in Father Christmas. All we need is a big red suit with a hood and some white fur trimming. A big white beard, a sackful of presents . . .' Her imagination ran on.

'And someone to wear it,' Grandad reminded her.

'Yes.' She stopped and looked him in the eye. 'Grandad . . .'

'Oh well, I don't know about that.' He coughed and stood up. 'I don't know that I'd be any good at dressing up. But you're right about the rest, Mandy. What we have to do now is mention it to a few people. I'm sure someone will volunteer straight away!'

'. . . I'll think about it,' Julian Hardy, the landlord at the Fox and Goose, listened to Grandad and Mandy's request. 'It's a bit short notice, but leave it with me.'

They'd left Animal Ark and walked into the village to look for a stand-in Father Christmas.

The landlord was an obvious choice. The plan was for the procession to start outside the pub with traditional carols and the collection, before it moved up the road to Beechtrees.

'Go on, Dad!' John Hardy pressed him to be a good sport. 'They need someone to say yes right now.'

'I can sort out a costume for you, and a long white beard.' Sara, Julian's wife, was all for it too. 'It'll suit you!'

'Ho-ho-ho!' The landlord practised his laugh. 'No, it's not me,' he said with a frown. 'Besides, we'll be busy in the pub.'

'Oh, Dad!'

'Julian, please!' Sara encouraged.

'Let me think about it.' This was his final word for now, so Mandy and Tom Hope pressed on, across the square to Walter Pickard's corner house.

'. . . Me, dress up as Father Christmas?' Walter snorted. He'd invited them into his kitchen, but now he evidently wished he hadn't. 'I never heard anything so daft!'

'Wait a minute. Think about it.' Grandad Hope stood there, perfectly reasonable. 'You're the right age for the job, Walter.'

'And so are you,' he retorted.

'Yes, but I'm more on the management side of

things. I'm a behind-the-scenes chap.'

Walter's eyebrows shot up. 'Oh, aye?'

'Yes. Whereas you're more the hands-on sort. I can just see you in a Father Christmas outfit, Walter. Besides, you wouldn't want to let everyone down, would you?'

Walter hummed and haahed. He coughed and shuffled. He said his rheumatism was bad, Tom was sick and needed full-time care.

'You won't be in the Fox and Goose for a pint tonight, then?' Grandad said with a sly wink at Mandy.

'Oh, I don't know about that,' came the instant response. He glowered at his visitors, unable to turn them down flat. 'Leave it with me,' he said as he showed them to the door. 'I'll mention it to Ernie. He's more your man!'

'. . . Father Christmas?' Adam Hope considered it. 'I'm a bit on the young side, aren't I?'

They'd bumped into him outside the post office on his way back from Sam Western's place. Customers came and went, rushing in to post late Christmas cards and to do last-minute errands. Mr Hope had stopped the Land-rover to offer Mandy and her grandfather a lift.

'I don't mind ringing Sam Western to ask if we can borrow his trailer,' he told them when he heard about the crisis. 'But I'm not so sure about playing the old man.'

'You'd be good at it,' Mandy pleaded. 'Wouldn't he, Grandad?'

'Brilliant. Just the right, friendly sort of chap.' But it looked as if Grandad Hope was beginning to think he would have to do the job himself after all. 'Look, if no one else seems keen, I suppose I could go home and get an outfit together before tomorrow night . . .'

'I might be out on call. Anything could happen between now and then.' Mandy's dad certainly wouldn't commit himself. 'Nice try, Mandy. I'll think about it.'

'What's the problem?' A familiar voice interrupted. Mrs Ponsonby appeared at the post-office door, ready to step into any breach. 'Do I take it that the real Father Christmas has gone missing?' She chortled at Mandy as she descended on to the pavement.

Mandy swallowed hard. Given half a chance, Mrs Ponsonby would step in and start bossing them around. 'He's stuck in Leeds,' she admitted. 'It's still snowing there. The roads are blocked.'

'Oh, dearie me!' And take charge Mrs Ponsonby did, standing there on the pavement with her two dogs, Toby and Pandora, both dressed in their little tartan jackets. 'We must do something!' She braced herself. The feathers in her red hat blew in the chilly breeze. Her round figure stood firm. 'We must find another!'

'Which is exactly what we're trying to do.' Mandy's grandad tried to get a word in.

Mrs Ponsonby swatted him away with her hand. 'Hush, Tom, I'm thinking . . . Yes, of course! Now look, you just leave it all to me!'

When Mandy and her grandfather had done everything they could in the village, they went back to Animal Ark. It was past teatime, so Grandad continued down the lane to Lilac Cottage to hatch his own plans, while Mandy went into the house, tired and hungry.

'Which do you want first; the good news or the bad news?' her mum asked.

'The good news.' Mandy sighed and kicked off her boots. 'Go on, tell me that it's stopped snowing in Leeds and the roads are clear. Don is on his way back.'

'If only.' Emily Hope gave her a quick hug. 'But Rudolph is definitely on the mend. His temperature's down and he's eating normally.'

'Thank heavens for that.' Now the Christmas procession wouldn't be a complete flop. Rudolph could be the star of the show.

'Rudolph saves the day, just like in the song.'

Adam Hope was on the phone. 'I'm ringing Susan Collins's dad to arrange for him to bring his trailer over first thing in the morning.'

'So what's the bad news?' Mandy asked warily. Her mum was dressed to go out into the snow in her hat and jacket.

'I just heard from Lisa Hastings at Beechtrees. Amber's still up on the roof.'

'Oh no! Didn't the food tempt her down?'

'Apparently not. And the temperature's dropped below freezing again. I said I'd go over to see if there was anything I could do.'

'I'll come!' Though she longed for a rest, Mandy immediately offered to help.

'Good. Come on, then. The sooner the better.'

So Mandy turned around, stuck her feet back into her boots and went with her mum.

'Tiring day?' Mrs Hope drove confidently down the narrow lane. The snow sparkled yellow under the headlights. When her four-wheel drive caught a low branch or a bush, a shower of soft snow fell to the ground.

Mandy nodded. 'Poor Amber. She's been up there for hours.'

'I know. And it's turned very cold again. I'm worried about hypothermia.' She glanced at Mandy. 'When body temperature falls below a certain level in an animal, or a person for that matter, it makes the victim sleepy. If it's bad, they become unconscious.'

'And Amber's only a kitten.'

'That makes it worse, I'm afraid. Kittens are more susceptible. They don't have as much body fat to protect them against the cold.'

Mandy bit her lip and tried not to think that far ahead.

Beechtrees came into sight as they drove past the Collins' house. The main road was busy with traffic driving home from work or from last-minute Christmas shopping in Walton. Soon the car pulled up outside the bungalow.

'There she is; she's still up there!' Mandy scrambled out of the car as she spotted a tiny dark shape on the long slope of the white roof. Mr Hastings stood in the front garden. A ladder leaned against the side of the house.

'Let's hope it's not too late.' Emily Hope carried her heavy vet's bag into the porch. She had a quick word at the door with Mrs Hastings.

'We're sorry to drag you out,' Alex's mother began, 'but we've tried everything, short of actually climbing on to the roof. It's very slippery. And besides, Jeremy's afraid that it would scare the kitten even higher and make her lose her balance.'

'We don't mind.' Mrs Hope gave a reassuring smile. 'Where's Alex?'

'She's in her room. She's worried sick about poor Amber. No one knows how the kitten got on to the roof, but Alex is convinced it's her fault for not taking better care of her. She's crying her eyes out.'

'Tell her to try not to worry.' Emily Hope stepped back from the porch, and together with Mandy went to join Mr Hastings at the foot of the ladder.

'It's no good.' He shook his head. 'Every time I climb up there, she just creeps further away. I don't want to scare her into making a false move.'

Mandy craned her neck to see the tiny kitten. She could just make out a sorry bundle of fur shivering on the roof. She heard a feeble miaow. Amber was too frightened to move a muscle.

'How cold will she be up there?' Mr Hastings asked, anxious but helpless.

'Very cold. She'll get frostbite if she has to stay any longer.' Mrs Hope made a quick decision. 'Mandy and I will have a go at getting Amber down, but meanwhile I think you should call the RSPCA. They have the right equipment to get up there. Explain the situation to them, and see if they can come out right away!'

He nodded and ran inside. As he opened the

door, Mandy caught a glimpse of William hovering in the hallway. It seemed he was curious to know what was going on, but was also trying to keep out of the way. The door closed again, and shut him inside.

'Let me go up the ladder, Mum,' Mandy said quickly. 'Amber knows me. She's more likely to come when I get up there and call her.'

Emily Hope checked the ladder. 'OK, but don't try anything risky when you get up there. I don't want you climbing on to the roof under any circumstances. Got that?' She knew Mandy would be willing to risk it unless she ordered her not to.

Mandy had to agree. She would have to rely on coaxing Amber down.

'Good luck,' her mum said, holding the ladder firm as Mandy set foot on the first metal rung.

She counted the steps; six, seven, eight. At nine, her head reached roof level. She peered up the snowy slope to the ridge. Amber sat and shivered against the chimney stack. Her eyes gleamed orange in the dark. 'Here, Amber!' Mandy edged up another rung. The kitten backed away.

'That's far enough, Mandy!' her mum warned from below. 'If she won't come when you call, we'll leave it to the RSPCA!'

Mandy leaned against the guttering and reached

out with both hands. Her legs had begun to tremble. The icy wind whipped up loose snow and blew it in her face. 'Amber, don't be scared. Come this way!'

In her confusion, Amber thought that Mandy's outstretched arms meant danger. She edged back again, almost lost her footing on the snow-covered ridge and half slipped from sight. Mandy gasped. With a struggle, the kitten found her balance and cowered against the chimney stack.

'Any good?' Mrs Hope called.

'No!' Mandy looked desperately along the treacherous surface. The roof was smooth and white except for two raised squares where windows had been built in for extra light. These too were snow-covered, but they gave Mandy an idea. 'I'm coming down!' Forcing her trembling legs into action, she climbed down the ladder.

'What next?' Emily Hope looked at her watch. 'Where's the RSPCA got to?'

'I'm going to try from inside!' Mandy ran to explain to Mr and Mrs Hastings. 'Can you open the roof windows from inside the house?'

Jeremy Hastings nodded. 'They work on hinges and lift up. Come and see!'

He led her to Alex's bedroom.

'Mandy, please get Amber down!' The little girl sat huddled on her bed, crying at the thought of Amber freezing to death.

Mandy put on a brave show of confidence. 'Don't worry, we'll get her back for you.' She was shocked by Alex's pale, tear-stained face, her tiny, distressed voice.

'Don't let her die, please!'

'Now Alex, we're all doing our best, love.' Jeremy Hastings looked round the room for something to stand on.

She sobbed quietly and hid her face as her dad put a chair in the middle of the room and began to lever at the snow covered window in the sloping ceiling.

Mandy waited impatiently, hoping that the noise wouldn't frighten the kitten outside.

'No good, it's frozen solid.' Mr Hastings gave up and jumped to the floor.

'What about the other one?' Mandy had seen the shape of a second window.

'In William's room!' He left Alex crying and ran next door, bursting in without knocking.

Mandy followed. What was William making of all this? She saw him on his bed, pale and silent, pretending to read a book, but obviously scared. She stood under the skylight while Mr Hastings ran for a chair to stand on. Looking down, she saw that the fawn carpet had a darker stain; a patch of wet about ten centimetres across.

William followed her gaze. He slammed his book shut and glowered.

Had water leaked in through the window frame? Mandy looked up. Or had snow drifted in through the open window? This window was lower, just out of reach. She shot another glance at Alex's brother, who went whiter still. His lip began to quiver as he heard his dad coming back.

'William?' It struck Mandy all at once; that was how Amber had got stuck on the roof. The boy had opened the window and put her there on purpose! Then he'd slammed it shut and locked her out!

'Don't tell!' he whispered, guilty, terrified.

Mr Hastings dashed in and put the chair over the wet patch without noticing it. He climbed up on it. This time, the window opened easily. He eased it up and propped it into position. 'Come on, Mandy, take a look. See if you can coax Amber down from here.'

Recovering from her shock, she stood on the chair and peered out. She was closer to Amber, but still not able to reach. The kitten saw her, but this time she didn't react. She blinked and shivered, but didn't try to escape.

Mandy knew the signs. This was worse than before; Amber was so cold that she was growing sleepy. But it was the kind of sleep before she fell unconscious and froze to death. 'Amber, here!' Mandy cried. She tried desperately to slither on to the roof.

'Careful!' Mr Hastings yelled.

Out on the road, an RSPCA van pulled up at last. From her vantage point, she could see two men rush into the Hastings' garden with special roof ladders. They scrambled up the side of the bungalow, one after the other, laid the roof ladder flat on top of the snow and pushed it into position.

Amber saw it and gave a cry. She darted away, along the ridge of the roof, almost slipped and fell.

'Watch out!' Mandy warned. The first man began to scale the roof. 'She might fall!'

But it was now or never. If the kitten stayed out any longer, she might die. Mandy hoped and prayed that the men would succeed where she had failed.

But terror jerked Amber into action. She made another run, further out of reach. She looked round, eyes wide with fright. There, just above, was an overhanging branch from one of the tall trees in the garden. The kitten saw it and crouched. The man hesitated. Then he lunged to grab her.

Amber jumped. She sprang up on to the nearest branch. It dipped and swayed. The kitten hung on.

'I've lost her!' the man shouted. Outside, someone else yelled, and the traffic on the road rumbled by. The dark shadow of the tree had swallowed Amber.

'Quick!' Mandy slid back into the bedroom, bringing a shower of loose snow with her. She ran out through the hall into the porch. Her mum stood with her bag, ready to treat the kitten. 'She's up in the tree. We can't see her!'

'Bring a torch!' Emily Hope told Jeremy Hastings. They ran to the base of the tree.

'Shine it up into the branches!' The RSPCA

man held his own torch. The yellow beams shone through the dark.

'She's up there somewhere!' Mandy whispered. 'She has to be!'

But though the RSPCA men brought their ladder and climbed once more, they couldn't find Amber.

'She can't just disappear!' Frantic, Mandy ran into the road to see if she could see Amber from out there. The moon shone through the bare branches; there was no sign.

'Watch the cars!' Mr Hastings warned.

Mandy kept close to the side, searching the road just in case the kitten had lost her balance and fallen. Again, nothing!

Amber's mighty leap from rooftop to tree had ended in mystery. They searched and searched, but the kitten seemed to have vanished into thin air!

6

'What shall I tell Alex?' Mr Hastings asked as he clicked off his torch.

They felt empty and cold. The men from the RSPCA had stacked their ladders on top of the van and driven away from Beechtrees.

'I think we should tell her the truth.' Mandy's mum offered to help him explain.

They trudged into the house. Mrs Hastings brought Alex from her room and they broke the news that Amber was lost. There were tearful questions; 'How can she be? Isn't she stuck on the roof? Where is she now?' The grown-ups were gentle, but they had to admit that they had failed.

'At least until it gets light,' her mum told her. 'Then we can begin to look again. We'll be able to see more in the daylight.'

'But it's so cold!' Alex shivered with fear. 'Why can't we try to find her *now*?'

'We *have* looked for a long time,' Mr Hastings began. But he saw the look in Alex's green eyes. 'OK, I'll try again.'

Mandy said she would go with him, while Mrs Hastings and her own mum did their best to calm Alex.

'William, come and give us a hand,' Jeremy Hastings called from the front porch.

The boy's bedroom door opened slowly. When he saw Mandy, he closed it quickly again.

'What's got into him?' His father was impatient. 'As if we didn't have enough to worry about, without William going into a sulk.'

Mandy waited while he went to fetch his son. William appeared reluctantly, grumbling about having to go out in the cold. He avoided Mandy's gaze.

'It isn't even my kitten,' he complained, as his dad made him put on his jacket and boots.

'But Alex is upset. Don't you want to help us find Amber for her sake?'

William screwed his mouth up tight. He said nothing.

'Come on, try and put someone else first for a change.' Mr Hastings handed them each a torch and they went outside. They searched behind bushes along a low wall, across the lawn where the two snowmen still stood, gleaming white in the moonlight.

'Let's look for paw-prints,' Mandy suggested. She directed her torchbeam along the ground. 'If Amber did fall out of the tree and manage to run off, we should soon be able to pick up her trail.'

For a while, their search had a new purpose. Surely Mandy was right; the kitten would have left some evidence in the snow. But the minutes ticked by. They looked on the lawn, then under the beech tree for the telltale prints. Mr Hastings even went up his ladder to investigate the roof for fresh signs. He had no luck up there either.

'I'm freezing!' William moaned. He sniffled and whined. 'My toes hurt! I can't feel my fingers!'

'Well, just think how cold Amber must be!' Mr Hastings refused to let him retreat into the house. 'Now go with Mandy and look on the road. Watch out for cars!'

'It's all clear,' Mandy called. She stood at the gate, shining her torch along the wall top where the tree branches hung over the road. 'Can you see any prints?' she asked William.

He scowled. 'No. And it's not my fault if the

stupid cat goes missing! Why can't Alex look after her properly?'

Mandy bit her tongue. She hated it when people called animals stupid. All of a sudden she had to say something. 'Listen, William!' She pulled him to one side and whispered urgently.

'Let go! What?'

'Are you sure it's not your fault that Amber went missing? What about that patch of melted snow on your carpet?'

'Don't blame me. I was only trying to rescue the stupid thing before Mum went and rang you lot!' He looked at her at last, eyes flashing angrily. 'Anyway, I know you won't believe me. No one ever does. They never blame Alex. It's always me!' He pulled his sleeve free and ran into the garden. Mandy quickly followed.

She saw William jump the low wall on to the lawn. He headed straight for the snowmen which he and James had built, threw himself at the nearest one and began shoving and kicking it until it toppled and shattered. It lay in frozen lumps. Soon he had destroyed the second one too.

'There!' He rounded on her, as his father came running down the path. 'That's what I think of stupid snowmen. And I hope you never find Amber! I hope she freezes to death!'

★ ★ ★

'He didn't really mean it,' Mrs Hope explained as she drove Mandy home.

'He sounded as if he did.' Mandy had been shocked by the outburst. In the end, Mrs Hastings had come out and taken William inside.

'He is only seven, remember. And his family has a lot of problems at the moment.'

'Yes, and William's making them worse.' Mandy couldn't forgive his cruel taunt about Amber. She sat looking out at the snow-covered hillside, staring disaster in the face. For one thing, there were the snags over Father Christmas. Gran and Grandad's fund-raising treat could well fall completely flat. For another, Alex was so upset about Amber that she might be too ill to enjoy the procession even if it did take place. And then of course, there was the kitten out all night in the cold.

'I'm sure he doesn't mean to make things worse,' her mum insisted. 'I don't think he can help it, poor boy.' She swung down their lane, talking things through. 'It must be hard for him, having a little sister who gets all the attention. Alex is ill, so naturally her mum and dad worry about her. They don't have much time to spare for William at the moment. I expect he feels left out.'

'Jealous?' Mandy considered it for the first time. 'But that didn't mean he had to go and spoil the snowmen. That doesn't make sense.'

'Sometimes things don't make sense.' They turned into their own drive and pulled up in the yard.

'Mum . . . ?' Frowning, Mandy unclicked her seatbelt. 'I know what you mean. William's getting his own back.'

'Yes. But he's having to take it out on things that never did anything to him in the first place. Like the snowmen.'

'And Amber?' Mandy wondered out loud. William had denied it, but the suspicion lingered that he was the one who had put the kitten on the roof.

'Possibly.' Mrs Hope listened quietly to the full story, as Mandy saw it. She sighed. 'Oh dear, I hope not. The poor boy must be feeling wretched.'

'Poor *Alex*, poor *Amber*!' If it was true, William had taken out his problem on the thing his sister loved best. And now an innocent animal was suffering because of it.

'Cheer up!' Adam Hope greeted them with a smile. 'Don't tell me you didn't see them out in the yard?'

Mandy shook her head wearily. 'No. Who?'

'Not who; what. The van and trailer. Don's back!'

'Och aye, I'm back all right.' The wiry

Scotsman came downstairs in T-shirt, jeans and bare feet. 'I've had a long, hot bath and now I'm ready to put my feet up in front of the TV.'

'Is Dasher with you?' It took a while to sink in. The last Mandy had heard was that the trailer was stuck in a snowdrift outside a Leeds hospital.

'Aye, and young James. All home safe and sound.' Don's face was shiny red after his bath. 'Now where did I put those trainers?' He scratched his head and began to search the kitchen.

'But how did you get here?' For a moment Mandy had a vision of the reindeer rising magically above the rooftops, drawing the sleigh.

'The snow-ploughs dug us out. They did a great job. By teatime they had the traffic moving again. We couldn't get a message through to you, so we headed for home. It's a good wee story, though.' He chuckled over it. 'Now where *did* I put those shoes?'

'At least I won't have to get dressed up in that red suit.' Mr Hope sounded relieved. He made Mandy sit down to a big plateful of beans on toast. 'You had us worried for a while, Don. Mandy's grandad has been all over the village trying to round up a stand-in.'

'And no one wanted to do it,' Mandy added. She tucked into her supper, glad that at least one of the major crises was over. 'Everyone said, "Let me think about it", which means, "No", doesn't it? But anyway, Rudolph's better and you're back.'

'No problem!' Don was cheery as ever. 'Maybe I left them in my bag,' he muttered to himself. He shuffled off in bare feet, upstairs to the spare room. They heard a few thumps and clomps as he came back down; shoes on but unlaced, and wearing a puzzled frown. 'That's not like me. I'm usually a very organised sort of person!'

Mandy rolled her eyes at her mum and dad. Don was many good things, but organised wasn't one of them. 'What have you lost?'

'Och, I wouldn't say "lost" exactly. More

mislaid. Aye, but I could have sworn I put them in my bag.'

'Your shoes? They're on your feet, Don.' Mandy broke it to him gently.

'Och, no, not my shoes. No, I'm talking about Father Christmas's clothes; the old gentleman's best red suit and black boots. I told him I'd spruce them up for Christmas Eve, so he left them with me. I've looked, and I can't find them anywhere!'

'He left them at the hospital,' Adam Hope confirmed as he came in to say goodnight to Mandy. 'The nursing manager just called and left a message. Father Christmas's suit is neatly folded on a bed in an empty side ward!'

Mandy made a noise halfway between a groan and a giggle.

'Yes, and you thought *I* was absent-minded!' He sat down for a moment on the edge of her bed. 'Your mum says you've had a hard day?'

She nodded. 'We looked everywhere for Amber, Dad, but we just couldn't find her. What do you think can have happened to her?' She knew that she wouldn't sleep for worrying.

Her dad shrugged. 'I don't know for sure, but let's try and work it out. Because one thing's for sure; a cat really can't just vanish. So, first off, you say she definitely jumped off the roof?'

'Yes, into the tree by the wall. We saw her land, but it was so dark among the branches that we lost sight of her.'

'And she's absolutely definitely not still up there?'

'No. So where can she be?'

'Well . . .' He spoke gently. 'We have to face the fact that Amber might have fallen.'

Mandy scrunched up her face and closed her eyes. She didn't want to hear this.

'No, listen, love. Say she did fall; after all, it was dark and she was very frightened. But you know cats have this amazing ability to land on their feet. We call it a head-on–body righting reflex.'

She opened her eyes to look at him. 'Meaning what?'

'It works like this. A cat falls from a height. First it twists so that the top of its head faces upwards. Then the neck and body line up in the reflex action so that the cat falls feet first. It only takes milliseconds, and lo and behold, she lands safely. One of her nine lives is saved!'

Mandy took a deep breath. 'Do you think that's what happened to Amber?'

'It's possible. She falls and lands the right way up, no damage done. Then as quick as she can she darts for cover, waits for all the fuss to die down.'

'Yes. Maybe she didn't like the torches and all

the noise.' Mandy pictured the kitten tucked safely out of harm's way, sheltered from the wind and waiting for the all-clear. Tomorrow morning the Hastings would open their front door and discover her, sitting on the mat and miaowing for her breakfast. 'I just hope she found a nice warm place to hide.'

'Me too.' Her dad stood up and turned off the light. 'After a day like today, we deserve a bit of luck. So try not to worry too much, OK?'

The door closed and left the room in darkness. Mandy tried to sleep. But one thing bothered her. If her dad was right, and Amber had landed safely, why hadn't they found any paw-prints in the snow? Mandy tussled with the problem until well after midnight. No paw-prints, no evidence, nothing. Poor little Amber; it seemed that she had simply been spirited away.

7

Gran turned up at Animal Ark before breakfast, armed with scissors, sewing-pins and an armful of old red curtain material. 'We'll just have to make do and mend!' she cried, seizing hold of Don. She measured him for a replacement Father Christmas suit. 'I expect Santa Claus is about the same size as you,' she said with a wink.

'Aye, though he's a wee bit fatter around the waist.' Don patted his stomach.

As usual, Mandy played along. She helped Gran get him ready for the grand procession that evening.

They laid the fabric flat on the kitchen table,

cut and shaped it, then Gran began to sew to the whirr of the machine, making tucks, seams and fastenings. By nine o'clock, Don was trying on the finished article.

'Beard?' Gran stood back to judge the effect.

'Cotton wool!' Mandy ran to the surgery. She dived through the busy waiting-room, grabbed a pack from the cupboard, and raced back to the house. By hook or by crook they would be ready for the big event.

'Boots?' Gran was almost finished. The beard was a miracle of cardboard, glue and cotton wool, with elastic loops to hook over the ears.

'Dad's wellies!' Mandy sprang to fetch them. Then, when they were satisfied and Don had gone outside to groom Rudolph and Dasher so that they would look their best for that evening, she rang James to see if he would come along to Beechtrees with her.

'What time is it? Have you rung them yet?' James inquired sleepily.

'No, not yet.' Mandy had been putting it off. 'And they haven't rung us either.' Her hopes that Amber would turn up on the doorstep of the bungalow were fading. She knew that the Hastingses would have telephoned with any good news about the kitten. 'I wondered if you would come and help us look.' She would be glad if he said yes. James was brilliant in a crisis. He kept a clear head and always came up with bright ideas.

'Sure. What time?'

'In half an hour.'

'See you there.' He was alert now, and didn't waste time talking.

In fact, he was at the bungalow before her. When Mandy arrived, he was already looking for the lost kitten with Mrs Hastings. Mr Hastings had gone to work at the tennis club, and William and Alex were inside.

'How is she?' Mandy asked.

'Not quite so upset as yesterday. But she's very sad,' Mrs Hastings told them. 'I can't think of anything to cheer her up. She's completely lost interest in Christmas.'

Mandy knew how Alex must feel. Even making Father Christmas's outfit with Gran hadn't stopped her from worrying about Amber. 'Shall I go in and see her?'

'Would you mind, Mandy? You're the only person Alex is interested in talking to right now. I'm afraid she sees you as some kind of heroine, like Superwoman!' Mrs Hastings gave a sad smile and led Mandy and James through the hallway.

James stayed in the kitchen while Mandy tiptoed into Alex's quiet room. The curtains were drawn, and a dim lamp shone. All around the walls, pictures of animals seemed to stare down at the sick little girl who lay motionless in bed.

'Hi, Alex.' Mandy sat close by. There was a full glass of water on the bedside table, next to an unopened book.

Alex turned her head. When she spoke, her voice was a whisper. 'Hello, Mandy. Guess what, I don't think Father Christmas read my letter.'

'Why not?' Mandy saw now what Mr and Mrs Hastings meant when they insisted that Alex must be kept calm. Being upset drained her of her strength. She lay white as a ghost.

'I wrote and asked him for a collar for Amber; one with a little bell.'

'Well, you never know.' She tried to sound cheerful. 'He might bring you one. He hasn't delivered his presents yet, remember!'

Alex's eyes filled with tears. 'No, but if he got my note, he'd know I've got a kitten. Then he wouldn't let Amber get lost, would he?'

'I don't think even Father Christmas can do anything about a kitten going missing,' Mandy explained gently.

'But he knows everything! He knows what we'd all like for Christmas. He can even fly through the air with his reindeer. He must know about Amber!'

Mandy nodded. 'Well, maybe he does.'

Alex had a sudden idea. She wiped her eyes and looked at Mandy. 'Yes, and maybe he's looking after her for me! That could be where Amber is right now – with Father Christmas!'

'I hope so,' Mandy whispered. Before Mrs Hastings came in to give Alex her medicine, Mandy crept out of the room to join James in the kitchen.

After a few minutes Mrs Hastings followed. 'She's sleeping,' she reported. 'It's an extra strain on her heart when she's upset. She isn't strong enough to take it.' It was Alex's mother's turn to brush away a tear.

'Come on, let's start,' James suggested, ready to take up the search. They went out on to the porch.

'I dread what sort of time we'll have if we don't find this kitten.' Mrs Hastings scanned the trampled lawn. 'We've been over and over the ground, but there's still no sign.'

James agreed. 'I thought we might find prints in the snow, but it's all trodden down, so even if there was a track last night, it's disappeared by now.'

'I did look,' Mandy told him. 'And I couldn't see one. William and I even searched out on the road.' She glanced at the house to see the small, pale face and ginger hair of Alex's brother staring solemnly at them through the window.

187

James studied the beech tree where Amber had last been seen. Then he went out to look at the road, which was quiet at this time of day. He stood under the overhanging branches and looked up, pushing his hair from his forehead. 'Who saw her up there?'

'Let's think; me, Mum, Mr Hastings, and the two men from the RSPCA.'

'And the people driving by,' James suggested. 'If Amber managed to scramble down the tree on this side, then ran off, maybe someone in a car caught sight of her as well?'

Mandy nodded. 'All we need is one clue to find out which way she went. But how do we find out if anybody saw her?'

'We could ask in the village. There would be plenty of people around on Christmas Eve, doing their last-minute shopping. It's worth a try.'

Mrs Hastings agreed. 'You two go and ask. I'll stay here and make some notices to stick up on trees and gateposts to say we've lost a kitten. I'll get Alex and William to help me.' She seemed glad to have something to do.

So Mandy and James went into Welford. They called at the McFarlanes' and the Fox and Goose. They saw James's dad talking in the square to Mrs Collins. They saw Ernie Bell and Walter Pickard.

'Tom's right as rain!' Walter called. 'Back

to normal, as bossy as ever!'

They passed the message; the Hastingses' kitten, Amber, was lost in the snow. Had anyone seen a stray tortoiseshell with bright golden eyes? Each time the answer came back: 'No, sorry. But we will keep a lookout!' Even the people who remembered driving past the bungalow at about the right time hadn't seen a thing.

They asked the Parker Smythes and Sam Western, as well as the farmer from Greystones, David Gill. All promised to do their best, but they shook their heads as if to say, 'What chance does a little kitten have out in the freezing cold at this time of year?'

By lunchtime Mandy and James had done all they could. They headed back, past the square, where Julian Hardy from the pub was stringing up big Christmas lights. 'Ready for Father Christmas,' he said. 'I hear everything's going ahead?'

Mandy nodded. Her legs were weary from tramping through the snow. And so far, all for nothing. They were no nearer to finding Amber. She forgot to mention to Mr Hardy that Don McNab and Dasher were back in Welford, ready for tonight's procession.

'Sara's busy baking mince-pies. And John's made christingle candles for the kids. The vicar's bringing a tape of Christmas carols, and I'll rig up loudspeakers so we can all sing along.'

Everyone was pulling out all the stops in aid of Alex's lifesaving trip to America. Mandy and James watched for a while, then went on, deep in thought. 'You know something?' Mandy said, 'Unless we find Amber, I don't think Alex will go!'

'For her operation?' James began to see how important the missing kitten was. 'You mean, she's just too upset?'

Mandy sighed and nodded. 'And too ill to travel. Come on, we'd better go and see what's happening.'

'If only *I*'d seen something.' James strode along beside her. 'Don and I drove along this road yesterday teatime, on our way back from Leeds.'

'Along with a hundred other cars.' She was beginning to feel that it was like looking for a needle in a haystack.

'Well, it looks like William is trying to help at last.' James spotted him in the garden. William climbed the wall and stood, watching them approach. As they drew near, he dropped to the ground and ran to meet them.

'Alex is even more sick! They've fetched the doctor.' His eyes were wide and scared. 'Did you find the kitten?'

Looking up the drive, they saw a red car, and

the front door of the bungalow standing open. A tall woman came out carrying a dark bag. She stopped to talk earnestly to Mrs Hastings. The moment William spotted them, he ducked behind the wall. 'That's her,' he told them. 'That's the doctor!'

They waited until the woman had got into her car, backed out of the drive and driven off. By this time, William was shaking from head to foot.

'I never meant her to get sick!' He trembled and fought back the tears, refusing to go any nearer to his house. The front door was closed, the bungalow strangely quiet.

'Just like you never meant Amber to get lost in the snow?' Mandy asked quietly.

James stepped back in surprise. William hung his head. 'I only wanted her to be on the roof for a bit. I didn't know she wouldn't come down again.' He mumbled and choked over how his plan had gone wrong.

'You mean, *you* put Amber up there?' James was stunned.

Mandy nodded. 'I thought so. Listen.' She knew the whole story would soon come tumbling out.

'Yes, but I thought I could get her down again. They'd all be looking for her, and I'd be the one who saved her, see?'

'But it didn't work out.' Instead of rescuing

the kitten and being the hero, William had to watch Amber climb out of reach on the roof, then get too scared to move, slowly growing colder and colder as night fell. 'Why didn't you tell someone?'

'I was frightened,' he confessed. 'I thought Amber was going to die because of me.' Tears welled up and rolled down his cheeks.

'Look, never mind that now.' James knew there was no point crying over it. 'At least we know how it happened.'

Mandy wondered how James could be so kind. She found it hard to forgive William. But the little boy looked miserable as he realised just what

he'd done, and Mandy remembered what her mum had said; William was feeling left out. He was a lonely child who knew he'd done wrong. 'We won't tell anyone,' she whispered. 'Don't cry any more. Just help us to find Amber!'

William sniffed and dried his eyes on his cuff. 'I don't want to go in,' he pleaded.

'OK.' James was practical. 'Let's stay outside and look.'

'Again!' Mandy stood at the gates, hands on hips. It almost drove her mad to think how often they'd gone over this ground since Amber had disappeared.

But William shook his head. 'No!' he insisted. He pulled back as James tried to persuade him to come into the garden.

'Why not? The least you can do is help us look!' For the first time, James sounded cross.

'I can't. Anyway, there isn't any point!'

Mandy turned. 'Don't, James. What's wrong, William?' She suspected there was more to come.

'Amber's not here.'

'How come? Did you see what happened?'

Slowly he nodded. 'I was looking out of the window. She was in the tree. Everyone was using ladders and torches, but I knew it wasn't any use.'

'Why not? What did you see?' She longed to

shake the truth out of him, but she forced herself to be patient.

William stood at the roadside, pointing up at the tree. 'She was in that branch, there. I saw her. I shouted, but you didn't hear because there was too much noise.' There was a long pause. 'Amber fell.'

'Where? Into the road?' James was the one to prompt him, as Mandy held her breath.

'No. She fell on to a sort of truck. I saw her slip from the branch. The next second the truck went past the gate and I saw Amber on top of it, hanging on.'

'Alive?' Mandy gasped.

He nodded. 'The truck drove on. I couldn't stop it.'

James's mind flew ahead. Mandy was dazed, but overjoyed that Amber had survived the fall. 'What kind of truck?' he asked.

'A grey one. It was a kind of trailer.'

James stared. 'What was pulling the trailer?'

Mandy grabbed James's arm, waiting in suspense for the reply.

'A big van, a dirty white one. It was covered in snow. I'd never seen it before.'

They gasped. 'Don!' they said together.

'The reindeer's trailer!' Now, at this moment, Mandy could have hugged William. Here was the clue they needed. 'Amber fell on top of it!'

'It looks like it,' James breathed. 'The kitten must have driven home with Don and me!'

'To Animal Ark!' Mandy cried. 'Oh, James, Alex was right; Father Christmas has been looking after Amber all along!'

8

'William saw what happened to Amber!' Mandy told Mrs Hastings, so excited that she could hardly get the words out. 'At last we've picked up a lead we can follow!'

Mrs Hastings went straight away to tell Alex the latest news while William slipped quietly back into the house. 'I won't get her hopes up too high just yet,' Alex's mum said. 'But at least this should help to cheer her up.'

'We hope!' James whispered to Mandy as they set off down the road, as fast as they could, towards Animal Ark.

★ ★ ★

Back at Animal Ark, Mandy and James found the reindeer's trailer standing in the yard. Its doors hung open and the ramp was down. They nearly fell over themselves getting inside it. Their feet thumped up the ramp, and they almost tumbled over.

But, once inside, they soon realised that the dark trailer was empty. Mandy had longed for it to be simple. She had hoped Amber had clung on to the top of the trailer and during the journey home had clambered inside to safety − to spend the night in the warm straw. But no; the trailer was bare. No kitten, not even any straw.

'Don must have cleaned it out,' James said, his voice flat.

'Let's make sure.' Mandy took one last look round, then went out, and hoisted herself up on to a ledge to look on top. There was no kitten there, but something caught her eye. 'James, come and look at this!'

James joined her. Together they peered on to the snowy roof of the trailer.

'See there.' She pointed.

Frozen into the deep snow was a trail of paw-prints which led from a scuffed patch. 'You think that's where Amber fell?'

'Yes, then she crept to that far edge, there.'

'Well, at least we know William's telling

the truth,' James agreed. 'But that's not to say that Amber stayed there all the way back here.' He jumped down and tried to think what to do next.

'Let's ask Don if he knows anything.' Mandy caught sight of him in the compound with the two reindeer. 'Don!'

He waved as she ran across.

'Don, did you just muck out the trailer?'

'I did.' He hummed cheerfully. Rudolph was enjoying a grooming session ready for the big night. Dasher nibbled at a dish of sugar beet.

'Did you see anything in there?' Again she was in such a rush that the words tumbled out. 'Like a kitten, for instance?'

'Whoa, slow down!' His eyes crinkled with amusement. Mandy hopped from foot to foot, and now James came running. Rudolph grunted and nudged at Don's hand. 'Aye, steady on, Rudi. I haven't forgotten you!'

'A brown and black tortoiseshell kitten with amber eyes!' Mandy gave a full description to a mystified Don.

'Aye, as it happens, I did.'

'Oh!' Mandy clasped her hands together. 'Oh, Don, where is she? What did you do with her?'

'Well, I didn't do anything with her.' He scratched his head. 'I went into the box and there she was curled up in the straw, cosy as you like. Cheeky wee thing.'

'You didn't chase her away?' James asked anxiously.

'Och, what do you take me for? It was a pity to disturb her; she'd found a grand spot for a wee nap. No, I went off to fetch her a saucer of milk, but wouldn't you just know it? The minute I turned my back, off she ran.' He shrugged and started again on Rudolph's thick coat. 'She's a wicked wee cat, right enough.'

Mandy stared. 'She ran off?' she faltered.

'Aye, but don't worry. Kittens don't stray far from home. You'll soon have her back safe and sound.'

'No,' James cut in. 'Amber doesn't belong to Mandy. She doesn't live here at Animal Ark.'

'But I thought you said you were looking for her?' Don stood up straight and wrinkled his forehead.

'For someone else,' James explained. 'Did you see which way she ran?' Of course, Don couldn't realise how important this was. They'd been so near to finding Amber, yet now they'd lost her again.

He sighed. 'I didn't. She nipped away when my back was turned. I just got on and mucked out as usual. I never gave the wee cat a second thought.'

Mandy hid her disappointment. 'Never mind. Thanks, Don.'

'Och, I've a feeling I've let you down,' he apologised.

'No.' She managed to smile. 'At least we know Amber was here.'

'How long ago?' James fitted together all the information he could gather.

'Half an hour. Maybe a wee bit longer.'

Mandy nodded at James. 'Then she can't have gone far!' she said, jutting out her chin and looking across the yard. The hunt for Amber was on.

In the small village of Welford, news of the missing kitten travelled fast.

'Little Alex Hastings is ill with worry, poor child!' Mrs Ponsonby spread the word. She'd heard it from Emily Hope when she went into the surgery with snuffly Pandora. She told Mrs McFarlane that the kitten was still alive. 'Isn't that wonderful? And wouldn't it be the best Christmas present in the world if we all helped to find her?' Warm-hearted in spite of her bossy manner, Mrs Ponsonby raised a search party.

'I suppose I've nothing better to do.' Ernie Bell hid his willingness to help beneath a grumpy surface. He picked up a shovel from his garden shed and set off for Animal Ark, ready to dig through snowdrifts and do his very best.

Walter Pickard, not to be outdone, went with him. 'We can't have the little lass making herself poorly over it, can we?'

And John Hardy, the serious, studious son of the landlord, went along with Susan Collins. Even Brandon Gill, the shy boy from Greystones Farm, got to hear about Amber and tramped across the snowy fields to Mandy's house. Soon a dozen people, young and old, were helping James and Mandy in the search for Amber.

'We must spread out in different directions!' Mrs Ponsonby was wearing a bright pink anorak with a white fake-fur trim. She had a master plan. 'Mandy and James have checked the house thoroughly, so we can be sure that the kitten has gone further afield. We will split into twos and search the lane with a fine-tooth comb. Now Mandy, please give a detailed description.' She clapped her hands smartly. 'Attention everyone, please!'

Mandy blushed as she gave the information. 'Amber is a black and brown tortoiseshell with golden-orange eyes. Her tail is mostly black. There's a flash of white on one back leg. She's five months old.' Even as she spoke, she realised that the short daylight hours would soon draw to a close. They must get the search underway as soon as possible.

They left it to Mrs Ponsonby to divide people into pairs. 'Walter, you come along with me!' she instructed, after she'd sent all the others off.

Mandy raised her eyebrows. James breathed a sigh of relief. Walter got no chance to object.

'Go on, Mandy. You and James head for Lilac Cottage. See if your grandparents have seen or heard anything useful!' Mrs Ponsonby implied that the two of them were slacking.

They shot off, leaving Walter to be bossed around by her, passing Brandon and Susan who had been sent to look in the field opposite Animal Ark.

'Here!' Susan said, suddenly excited. She pointed to a track that led right across the field. 'A set of footprints!'

James and Mandy jumped the ditch to peer over the wall.

Brandon stopped to examine them. 'A fox,' he said quietly, shaking his head.

'Oh, Brandon, are you sure?' Susan was dismayed. She clung on to her discovery. 'But they look like cat prints to me!'

'Fox,' he said stubbornly. 'They're too heavy for a kitten.'

Susan sighed and gave in. Mandy and James

jumped back into the lane and went on. The snow still lay deep and pretty as a Christmas card along all the wall-tops and gates, weighing down the dark tree branches. By the time they reached the cottage, they'd passed Ernie, John Hardy and Mr Hastings, who'd rushed over from work the moment he heard the news.

'Thanks, you two!' He raised his head and called after him. 'You don't know how much we appreciate this!'

'Thank us later,' Mandy told him.

'When we find Amber!' James added.

At Lilac Cottage Grandad stood holding the gate open for them. 'Come on. Your gran and I have been having a good scout around, but no luck so far, I'm afraid.'

It was the same old story; everyone doing their best but getting nowhere.

'That kitten certainly has a knack of vanishing!' Gran was in the front garden, looking under benches and behind bare trellises where, in the summer, roses grew.

'Poor thing. It must be a big cold world out here for her.' Grandad pictured her lost and frightened. It made James and Mandy concentrate even harder.

'Here, Mandy!' James called at last. His warm breath turned to clouds of steam as he trod carefully amongst Mr Hope's vegetable garden at the back of the cottage. 'Come and look!'

Mandy walked delicately between the mysterious white humps and clumps. Under the snow lay Grandad's precious rhubarb and fruit bushes. Her footsteps were the first to spoil the smooth surface of the carefully tended ground.

James crouched by a round water butt at the bottom of the garden. The barrel was covered over with a thick layer of ice, but it was the base that he was interested in. There, around the back of the barrel, leading along the garden boundary towards the house, was a beautiful, clear set of paw-prints!

'What do you think?' he breathed. 'Not a fox's this time?'

'Definitely not! Not so close to the house.' She followed the track to see where it led. 'Anyway, they're too small for a fox.'

Excited now, they followed the trail on to the patio. They lost it, then found it again. The prints lead along the patio, straight up to the sliding glass doors.

Mandy turned to James. 'What now?'

He shook his head. 'It looks like she went inside.'

'But who would let her in? Gran and Grandad would have mentioned it.' Doubts came to the surface; doubts that she didn't want to admit.

James pressed his face to the glass and peered inside. 'Uh, Mandy . . .' he said dully.

She forced herself to look. *Please let it be Amber!* she prayed. But there, sitting peacefully in his favourite armchair, carefully grooming behind his ears, was the sleek grey shape of Smoky, Gran and Grandad's own precious cat.

9

Smoky saw two surprised faces peering in at him. He opened his mouth in a great big yawn. Then he stood and arched his back, rousing himself from sleep.

For the first time ever, Mandy wasn't glad to see him. In fact, her heart gave a thud of disappointment. As Smoky leaped from his chair and came padding across the carpet towards them, tail up, ready to say hello, she turned away.

'No, wait a minute . . .' James chewed his lip. 'Maybe Smoky can help us!'

Mandy didn't see how. She stood on the patio, trying to get over this latest disappointment.

Grandad's garden, all covered with snow, with its bare apple trees and empty greenhouse, looked as bleak as she felt. Would they ever find Amber?

'Mandy, listen!' James insisted. 'This garden is Smoky's territory. He thinks it belongs to him.'

She agreed. 'That's right. He keeps watch over it.'

'Just like Eric at home. He has a track that he follows, like the one by the fence. He kind of travels a network of paths on his home patch.' He knew that male cats were especially keen to keep invaders out.

Mandy began to see what he was getting at. 'So, if there's another cat around, Smoky would soon see him off.'

'Or *her*!' James suggested. He stared through the glass door at Smoky, who miaowed silently to be let out.

'You mean, if Amber is anywhere round here, Smoky would soon find out?'

James nodded. His eyes were wide with excitement behind his round glasses. 'What do you think?'

'It's worth a try!' Immediately Mandy seized the handle and slid the door open for Smoky to step out. 'Come on, Smoky. There's a good cat.' She stopped to stroke him and let him rub against her leg. He trod delicately into the snow, lifted one front paw and shook it.

James eased the door closed behind him. 'Just in case he prefers to run back inside into the warmth!' he whispered.

Smoky raised his head and looked around at the strange white world. His ears twitched and he followed the flight of a sparrow from Grandad's fence to the apple-tree. He flicked his tail and miaowed.

Mandy and James held their breath. They watched Smoky stalk towards the tree. He crouched by the gnarled trunk, staring up at the sparrow. The bird hopped and twittered in the branches above. As Smoky sprang for the trunk and his claws dug into the bark, the sparrow fluttered and flew off. Smoky dropped silently to the ground, disappointed.

When cats chased birds, they were like tigers, Mandy thought. Or like jaguars stalking through the jungle. Smoky settled low on the ground, haunches raised, tail flicking to and fro.

'What's he seen now?' James breathed. They didn't dare move, as Smoky marked out his territory and went prowling down the garden between the rows of snow-covered vegetables.

'Shh!' Mandy crept quietly after the cat. Smoky had picked up a scent. He padded round the water butt, set off on his track by the fence, sniffed again, then turned back in his tracks. He trotted smartly towards the greenhouse, stopped by a half-buried stack of upturned plant-pots and hissed.

They heard a tiny noise; a faint, frightened miaow. The fur rose along Smoky's back as he arched and let out a loud yowl. Mandy and James ran for the greenhouse as fast as their legs would carry them.

Yet, when they got there, expecting to find Amber cowering in a corner, there was only Smoky. He hissed and growled; the fur on his back standing on end as he arched and spat.

'Let's look inside the greenhouse!' Mandy dived for the door. She wrenched it open and peered inside. Empty shelves, empty plant-pots and trays. No kitten.

'Out here!' James listened again and traced the feeble miaow to the row of upturned pots. Some had toppled sideways and lay higgledy-piggledy round the back of the greenhouse. They were heavy clay pots, big enough for a kitten to get trapped inside . . .

Mandy rushed to help. The faint pleas grew louder. Smoky backed off. He sensed danger and crept to the edge of the vegetable patch, where he crouched, growling steadily.

'She must be stuck under one of these pots!'

James tried to reach down the narrow gap between the greenhouse and a tall fence. He overbalanced and fell against the glass panes. The whole greenhouse shook, but nothing broke. Instead, there was the sliding, rushing sound of heavy snow gliding down a smooth slope.

Mandy glanced up at the greenhouse roof. An avalanche of snow hung over the edge; a huge weight of snow just above James's head. 'Watch out!' She darted to pull him clear.

Just in time; the snow inched down the roof, hung for a second, then plunged to the ground in a shuddering thud. The kitten's cries were drowned as a mountain of snow buried her alive.

Gran and Grandad Hope came rushing from the front of the house. 'What was that?' Grandad had heard the noise. He stared in dismay at the solid mass of snow.

'Oh quick!' Mandy cried. 'Amber is under there! We heard her, then the snow fell on top of her. We need a spade to dig her out!'

In a flash Grandad headed for his garden shed. Gran rushed into the house to fetch the fireside shovel. Meanwhile, Mandy and James kneeled to scrape at the pile of snow. There was no sign of Smoky; he had fled across the garden in the rumble of falling snow.

Mandy dug with her bare hands. 'What if she's

been crushed?' The snow was heavy, packed into the gap between the fence and the greenhouse. It was about a metre deep.

'Don't think about it!' James scrabbled through the heap.

Soon Grandad came back with his spade. 'Try this!' He handed it to Mandy over James's head. She began to dig.

'Careful!' Gran warned. She gave the smaller shovel to James. He worked at the bottom of the pile, going in sideways.

At last Mandy's spade hit something solid. She scraped at the snow to reveal a cracked plant-pot, tumbled sideways under the avalanche. Digging carefully round it, she pulled it free.

'What's under there?' Grandad craned to see.

'More pots.' Mandy put the spade down and began to scoop with her hands again, while James dug his tunnel through the base of the pile.

'We've got to get air in there!' he gasped, his face red with the effort. 'Amber has to breathe!'

'Perhaps she's trapped under a pot, in a pocket of air,' Gran whispered.

'I hope you're right,' Grandad murmured.

Mandy pulled a second pot from the heap. It was broken in two. She thought she heard a faint cry from deep in the snow. Her heart leaped. 'Did you hear that?' In a frenzy she scraped at the snow, digging deeper and deeper.

'Yes!' James stopped tunnelling to listen. 'I heard it!'

'Oh be careful, Mandy!' Gran repeated. Any second the pile of snow could collapse and crush the kitten to death.

Mandy lifted out another shard of broken pot. The snow shifted and slid. She stopped, gathered her nerve and began again. This time she brought out a whole plant-pot, then another.

The cries grew louder, more insistent: *Miaow . . . miaow . . . miaow!*

Mandy scraped at the snow. She uncovered a pot. It was turned upside-down, like part of a

giant sandcastle made of snow. She did more careful scraping. The pot tilted then jolted back into position. The kitten wailed, then went quiet again.

'Ready?' Mandy breathed. She seized the pot with both hands, fingers frozen, arms trembling. She lifted it inch by inch so that the surrounding snow stayed in place. And there, under the plant-pot, hunched in a bedraggled ball, her orange eyes staring up at them, was Amber!

The news spread down the lane like wildfire; Mandy and James had found the kitten. Ernie, Brandon, Susan and Mr Hastings came running to Lilac Cottage. Mrs Ponsonby went to the village to proclaim the good tidings. Walter called in at Animal Ark to tell the Hopes. Soon everyone knew.

By this time Mandy had carried Amber into the house. She asked her gran for a towel and began to rub the kitten dry. Amber shivered and huddled inside the towel, mewing quietly.

'What about a hot-water bottle?' Grandad asked. They were still worried about hypo-thermia.

'No, she shouldn't have direct heat,' Mandy said. 'We mustn't warm her up too quickly. We just have to get her dry.' She said she didn't think there were any broken bones, but that Amber might have frostbite; she couldn't tell yet.

'Can she have warm milk?' Gran asked. They stood peering over James's head at Mandy kneeling on the kitchen floor with the kitten on her lap.

Mandy nodded. Soon Amber's fur was dry and fluffy. Gran brought a saucer of milk and Mandy set her gently on her feet. The kitten wobbled, then stooped to lap with her pink tongue. Mandy rested back on her heels and looked up at the worried faces. Her wet blonde hair was streaked across her cheek and neck. Her skin still tingled with cold. 'I think she's going to be all right!' she whispered.

A crowd had gathered outside the gate as Mandy wrapped Amber in a thick red blanket and took her out to Grandad's camper-van. They planned to drive to Beechtrees to deliver the kitten safely back home.

'Well done!'

'Isn't that great!'

'Oh, she's gorgeous!' There was a general murmur of approval at the sight of the rescued kitten.

Mandy let the helpers have a peep. There Amber sat, warmly wrapped up, purring like a little engine. She peered out from the red blanket at the row of strange faces, gave a puzzled miaow and snuggled deeper into Mandy's arms.

Grandad thanked everyone as he opened the gate. 'All's well that ends well!' He smiled and went to wait in the van.

Gran beckoned from the doorstep. 'Come on, Mandy. Don't keep that poor little girl waiting a moment longer!' She went to wave them off through the gate.

Mandy sat in the front with Amber; James sat in the back. Mr Hastings climbed in too, then slid the door of the camper-van shut.

They were on their way at last to give Amber back to Alex.

'Just in time,' Jeremy Hastings murmured. He stared out of the window across the valley at the twinkling lights of Welford village.

Just in time for Christmas, just in time for the grand procession; above all, just in time for Alex.

Mandy took Amber into Alex's bedroom. The kitten was still wrapped in the red woollen blanket. 'Look who I've brought,' she whispered.

Alex was still in bed, staring at the ceiling. Her hair shone coppery-red against the white pillows. She turned her head, hardly daring to believe her eyes.

Mandy tiptoed forward. 'It's Amber!'

'Really and truly?' Alex propped herself on her elbows. Then she sat up. 'Let me see!'

She unwrapped the blanket. Amber's round face peered out, eyes alert as she recognised the room. She sprang from Mandy's arms on to the bed, and went padding softly towards Alex.

The little girl held her arms wide open. She was speechless with delight. Amber stole straight into her arms. Alex wrapped them around the kitten, put her cheek against Amber's soft head and looked up at Mandy. 'Did Father Christmas tell you where to look?'

Mandy smiled. Alex's dream had come true. No more worries, no more tears. Now she could concentrate on getting better. 'In a way, yes, I suppose he did,' she said.

10

Don McNab was polite about Gran's specially made Father Christmas outfit. 'It's very good of you to go to all this trouble,' he said as she brought it into the yard at Animal Ark. He was busy transforming the trailer into the reindeer sleigh. 'But the old gentleman won't be needing it after all!'

Mandy and James were helping Don. It was seven o'clock; they had just half an hour to get the sleigh ready and to harness Rudolph and Dasher, before they were due in the village square. The evening was crisp and clear, a perfect Christmas Eve.

'Are you sure?' Gran was puzzled. As far as she knew, Don had left the proper outfit stranded in a hospital ward.

'Quite sure, thank you. I got a message to Father Christmas and he had a spare one specially sent down from Reindeerland!'

'Ah well.' She raised her eyebrows, then tucked the home-made suit back into her carrier bag. 'Perhaps it will come in useful another year.' Intrigued by the sleigh, she walked right round it. She admired the fibreglass side panels as James bolted them into place, and inspected the bulky pile of presents in the back. 'Lovely!' she told Mandy. 'I may be an old lady, but I confess I'm very excited!'

Mandy nodded. 'I know. I can hardly wait.'

'They're ready for you in the square,' Gran told Don. 'The fairy lights look beautiful. They've hung huge, old-fashioned lanterns outside the pub. And the music is already playing.'

'Is there anyone there yet?' Mandy asked. All they needed now for the procession to be a success was a huge crowd of people singing carols, all gathered to see Father Christmas and his sleigh.

'Quite a few. Your grandad and I are on our way back there now. Would you like a lift?'

But Mandy and James weren't quite ready. 'No thanks. We'll come down with Mum. Dad's had to go out on a call, so we'll meet him there.' She wanted to help Don hitch Rudolph and Dasher to the sleigh before they set off for the village.

So Gran said she would see them later. 'Don't be too long,' she warned, 'or you'll miss all the fun!'

But Mandy and James couldn't think of anything better than helping with the reindeer. They went to lead them out of the compound, smartly groomed, hooves clicking, white manes fluffed out. Their velvety antlers cast wonderful shadows across the yard.

'That's right, steady on!' Don encouraged as they entered them in between the shafts of the sleigh. 'Come on now, Dasher, back a wee bit further! That's it, Rudolph, you show him how it's done!' Slowly they eased the reindeer into position.

Dasher grunted and pawed the ground. The sleigh shifted behind him. Rudolph stood, the picture of patience, as if he sensed that their big moment had come.

'Grand!' Don was satisfied at last.

They stood back for the full effect. It was as good as they could possibly imagine; a gleaming sleigh with polished white sides, decorated in red and gold. There was a pile of presents stacked high on top, and two beautiful reindeer to draw it along the snowy lane. James glanced at Mandy, stuck both hands deep in his pockets, and raised his shoulders in a contented sigh.

'Right, you two!' Emily Hope called from the drive. 'We haven't got much time. I'll race you there!'

Mandy grinned. Her mum was dressed in a brown velvet hat with a fake-fur brim, a long, dark Russian-style coat and long boots. She looked too smart to race, Mandy thought. 'Can't we wait for Don?' she pleaded.

'No!' came the instant reply. Don was still busy checking the harness. 'Father Christmas doesn't like having folk around when he gets here. He's a wee bit on the shy side, like young James there!' He winked, and James blushed. 'You go on ahead,' he told them. 'Go and enjoy yourselves!'

So they had to say goodbye for now to Rudolph and Dasher.

'Twenty minutes to go,' Mandy's mum said as they set off on foot.

'I hope Dad gets back in time,' Mandy said. As luck would have it, the phone had rung and he'd had to go out. 'A vet's life,' he'd sighed. 'Always on call, always having to go and tend the sick and wounded!'

'Aah!' they'd cried. Mandy and James had felt truly sorry for him.

'Take no notice,' Emily Hope had told them. 'He's only playing for sympathy!'

So now they walked quickly along the lane in a threesome; Mandy, James and Mrs Hope. As they drew near the main street, they saw a string of parked cars, and heard carols playing over the loudspeakers. Then they saw the square. It basked in a glow of lights; yellow, red and green. A giant Christmas tree stood proudly in the middle, all lit up. A huge crowd was gathered round it.

Mandy felt a thrill of excitement. There were children running around, or perched on grown-ups' shoulders. There was Walter leaning on his garden gate, watching events, the Parker Smythes standing with Sam Western. Simon was talking to Jean, and Sara Hardy was dressed up in Victorian costume, wearing a long, hooped skirt and a shawl, taking round big trays of mince-pies.

Then Julian Hardy came out of the pub to conduct the singing. He handed out carol sheets. Everyone stood ready.

'There are hundreds of people here!' James tried to count, but gave up.

Mandy smiled at her mum, then slid in among the crowd. She took a song-sheet, on the look-out for her father, but instead she spied Gran and Grandad. They gave her a wave. She waved back, continuing to thread her way towards the front.

'While shepherds watched their flocks by night,
All seated on the ground,
The angel of the Lord came down,
And glory shone around!'

Faces in the crowded square were lit by lantern light. They opened their mouths and sang. The music floated into the night sky, a chorus of happy voices.

'Away in a-a man-ger,
No-o crib for a bed . . .'

Mandy sang her heart out. But where was her dad? Surely he should have finished his call by now. She edged sideways out of the crowd, to look down the road for the Animal Ark Land-rover.

But there, by the side of the Fox and Goose, she was waylaid by the strange sight of two Father Christmases arguing.

'Aye well, when I heard they were short of someone to do the job, I thought I'd better step in.' A grumpy voice growled from behind a fake white beard. The figure was hidden behind a red hood and cloak, but Ernie's trousers and sturdy boots were unmistakeable.

'Yes, and that was very kind of you!'

Mandy opened her eyes wide. Here too was a voice she recognised.

'It was really very thoughtful, Mr Bell. But now I think you should leave it all to me!'

This figure was short and round, with a big chest beneath the red, fur-trimmed coat. The hood was pulled well up, and the fruity voice muffled behind an outsize white beard. But it was true; Mrs Ponsonby was taking charge as usual. 'I know how to deal with small children, you see. You might frighten the poor little things. Now step aside and let me pass. We mustn't disappoint our public, must we?'

Ernie chuntered and grumbled. He wasn't going to give in without a fight. 'Look here, I had to borrow this lot from the wardrobe department at the Welford Players. They didn't let me have it for nothing neither!'

Mrs Ponsonby eyed the moth-eaten costume as if to say that Ernie had been robbed. She smoothed her own posh costume and stroked her beard. Mandy choked back a laugh.

'Break it up there!' Julian Hardy stepped in with a smile between the two would-be Father Christmases. The carols soared on. No one except Mandy had seen or heard the squabble. 'Didn't you hear? The real Father Christmas got back safely after all!'

'Surely not?'

'Well, I never!' Mrs Ponsonby and Ernie were stunned into silence. They unhooked their beards and threw back their hoods in the shadow of the pub wall. Suddenly the music changed. Bells jingled through the loudspeakers. All the children squeezed to the very front and peered up the street.

A roar of voices struck up with the first lines of Rudolph's song as Father Christmas's sleigh came into sight.

It was magical. Rudolph and Dasher pranced towards the square. The sleigh was all lit up with tiny white lights, silver bells jangled; it shone and sparkled as the reindeer drew near.

'Father Christmas!' the small ones gasped.

'Is he real?'

'Oh look, it's Rudolph!'

They all looked on in wonder.

Father Christmas sat up high, holding the reins; a round man with a red face and a big white beard. He was quite the most believable Father Christmas Mandy had ever seen.

Mandy felt James creep up alongside her. 'Doesn't Don look great?' she said.

'Shh!' He glanced round to make sure that no one had heard. 'Don't spoil it!'

They grinned at each other. Don McNab

certainly looked realistic as he stopped the sleigh in the square and stepped down. His loud voice boomed out a great 'Ho-ho-ho!'

'What do you think to him?' a voice asked quietly over their shoulders. 'The gentleman got here on time, just like I promised.' The voice had a definite Scottish accent.

'Don!' Mandy and James jumped sky-high.

'But you're . . .'

'You should be up . . .'

They stopped dead. Don grinned back. He stood there large as life in his thick jumper and jacket. 'Och no,' he protested. 'You didn't still think *I* was the old man! Do you not believe in the real Father Christmas, after all I've told you?'

They gulped.

'They do now.' Emily smiled as she passed by with a collection-box. She shook it in time to the tune. People reached deep in their pockets and gave generously. They said it was the best Christmas sleigh they'd ever seen.

When Mandy and James turned again to quiz Don, the Scotsman had melted away into the crowd.

Then there were gifts for the small children. They went up shyly one by one to whisper their Christmas wish. Father Christmas delved into the pile of wrapped presents and found the right sort.

The child went off hugging the parcel while mums and dads added money to the collection-boxes. The queue seemed to go on for ever, as kids with shining eyes got to stroke Father Christmas's reindeer.

At last all the carols had been sung, the presents given out. Collectors returned to the pub with their tins, where Gran and Grandad Hope counted up the total. More mince-pies were eaten, and then the crowd lined up along the street, ready for Father Christmas's sleigh to move on towards Beechtrees.

'He's due to make a special stop,' Mandy's mum explained. She stood between Mandy and James, waiting to hear Grandad's announcement of the grand total.

Grandad climbed on to the sleigh, sheet of paper in hand. He asked for quiet. The music faded, the excited voices died. Clearing his throat, he read from the paper. 'We have collected a grand total of eight hundred and seventy-nine pounds and thirty pence!' he announced proudly. 'Which, I'm delighted to say, means Alex and her family will be off to the States as soon as possible in the New Year! Well done, everyone, and thank you very much!'

Grandad got down from the sleigh to a round of applause. Then the crowd formed a long procession behind the sleigh.

'Come on.' Emily Hope put an arm round Mandy and James's shoulders. 'We can't miss the best bit!' She led them into the procession. They walked slowly to the jingle of bells and the click of the reindeer's hooves.

Before they knew it, they were outside the bungalow, underneath the tall trees. Father Christmas drew the reindeer to a halt. 'Ho-ho-ho!' he greeted the people at the house.

William appeared at the front window. He pulled back the curtain, gasped, then shot off. Soon the door opened and he stood in the porch, eyes bright, as Father Christmas beckoned him.

'Go on, William!' Mrs Hastings appeared behind her son and whispered softly. She put a hand on his shoulder and nudged him down the step. He ran down the path, shook hands with the figure in red and took a huge present from him. His mum stood by, smiling.

'Say thank you,' she prompted.

William could hardly see over his mysterious box. 'Thank you!' he whispered.

'And thank you, from Alex's dad and me too,' Mrs Hastings told Mandy. 'Your grandad tells me we can all go to America for Alex's operation.' Quickly she brushed a tear away as Jeremy Hastings hurried inside to fetch their daughter.

She took Mandy in her arms and gave her a great big hug.

And now it was Alex's turn. She came to the step with her dad, all wrapped up in coat, scarf and hat, carrying Amber. The kitten blinked at the lights on the sleigh.

'Here, give her to me,' Mr Hastings urged Alex.

As if in a daze, she handed Amber over and came slowly down the path. Father Christmas welcomed her with open arms. She smiled up at him; a dazzling, disbelieving smile. Then he lifted her clean off her feet and into the sleigh.

'Choose a present!' he boomed.

Alex pointed shyly to a small, round parcel. All the people who had helped to make this the best Christmas ever looked on, as she tore off the wrapping. Inside was a tiny blue leather collar with a silver bell. She held it up to show Mandy. 'Look! He must have got the letter. He brought this for Amber!'

Her dad came forward with a smile and handed her the kitten. Carefully Alex fitted the collar around Amber's neck.

'Would you like a ride?' Father Christmas let her and the kitten snuggle up close.

Wide-eyed, she stared up at him and nodded. 'Can William come too?'

'Plenty of room!' Father Christmas replied.

No sooner said than done, Jeremy Hastings hoisted his son up on to the sleigh.

Then Father Christmas took up the reins. 'Gee up, Rudolph! Gee up, Dasher!' The reindeer jerked once, then they were smoothly in step, clicking down the road.

Mandy and James ran to keep up. Behind them,

the crowd struck up another verse from 'Rudolph'.

Father Christmas joined in the song as he drove his sleigh along the snowy road. His deep voice boom-boomed through the clear night air.

Mandy and James stopped dead.

'You don't think . . . ?' James stared and stammered.

Mandy swallowed hard. 'No!' Father Christmas was fat and jolly, his beard was white. Her dad's was brown. 'Then again, where *is* Dad right this minute?'

They watched as the sleigh turned and came back towards them.

'Magnificent, eh?'

Mandy whirled round at the sound of the familiar deep voice. 'Dad!' He stood behind them, wrapped in scarf and hat.

'What's wrong? I said I'd be back in time for the celebrations, didn't I?'

'B-but!' She gazed again at the splendid red figure on the sleigh.

Adam Hope smiled broadly, and clapped his gloved hands. 'Merry Christmas!' he shouted above the jingling bells.

The sleigh drew up beside them, the reindeer grunted and shook their harnesses. Alex held tight to her kitten. She and William beamed at them.

Then Mr Hastings came and lifted the children down to the ground.

Finally, the old gentleman looked Mandy and James straight in the eye. He gave one of his booming ho-ho-ho laughs. 'Merry Christmas!' he said. They waved up at him, as he took the reins and drove off. 'Merry Christmas, everyone!'

LUCY DANIELS
Nutmeg

Illustrated by Bill Geldart

*For Lucy – a little cat with a big heart,
who is very much missed*

1

Nutmeg pushed her nose against the door. It moved slightly. She pushed again, harder this time and the door slowly swung open. *Should I go in?* she wondered to herself. Nutmeg had never been into this room before without her owner, Dan Brown – or his sister, Helen, or their mum and dad. But for some reason someone had left the door slightly open today.

There must be so many new places to explore and things to play with in there. It won't do any harm. I'll go in, just for a quick look, Nutmeg thought. Keeping her eyes and ears alert she sneaked into the room.

'Who's a pretty boy, then?' The squawk was so loud that it made Nutmeg's ears hurt and her heart patter inside her. She scuttled under a low table. She had forgotten Sailor!

Sailor was a very old, very large parrot that had belonged to Mrs Brown since before nine-year-old Dan, or his older sister, Helen, were born. Sailor was allowed outside his cage during the daytime. He had to stay in this room, but it was large and airy so Sailor had plenty of space to fly around in. Throughout the day, Sailor's cage sat empty at the side of the room, but its door was always left open. Regular as clockwork, the parrot made his way into the cage each evening. Sailor liked to feel safe at night while he slept. He liked the door of his cage to be closed, and a thick cloth thrown over it.

'Who's a pretty boy, then?' Sailor said again.

Nutmeg peeped out from the safety of her hiding place. She was not sure whether she should be frightened of him or not. He was so big! 'I'm a girl, actually,' she miaowed.

Sailor was perched on the back of a chair near his cage. He flapped his enormous wings and showed off the beautiful colours of his feathers — blue, red, green and yellow. Then he preened himself with his long, hooked beak, not taking his beady eyes off Nutmeg for a second. 'Who's a pretty boy, then?' he squawked again.

Nutmeg thought he was teasing her. 'I know my fur isn't as bright as your feathers,' she miaowed, 'but I'm proud of my golden-brown coat.'

Sailor just sat and stared at Nutmeg. She began to feel braver. *Never mind that nuisance of a parrot, I've come in here to explore*, she decided. She turned her back on Sailor and scampered across the room.

First she found a rather interesting wire. It trailed along the floor by the television. Holding it between her paws Nutmeg rolled over and over, getting herself thoroughly tangled up. She lay still for a moment, then wriggled her way out.

Looking around for the next game she saw Sailor glaring at her with his little black eyes. He had followed her across the room.

'Hello, Sailor!' he squawked.

Nutmeg tried to ignore him. She lay on her side on the thick fireside rug and began to wash herself the way Bracken, her mother, had taught her. She licked her front paws and brought them all over her face and ears, then she lifted her legs one by one. Finally, she washed her cream tummy and throat. That was better! If only that parrot didn't make so much noise!

'Hello, Sailor!' Sailor squawked. 'Hello, Sailor!'

Nutmeg's tail began to thump a slow steady beat on the carpet. Sailor was making her cross.

'Hello, Sailor!' Sailor squawked with an ear-piercing sound. 'Hello, Sailor!'

'Silly old Sailor!' hissed Nutmeg. With one swift movement she rolled over on to her feet and sprang at the parrot.

Sailor flapped his wings noisily and flew to the top of his empty cage where he sat screeching at full volume. 'Get off! Get off! Get off!' he cried out at the top of his voice.

There were thundering footsteps as Dan dashed

into the room, followed by his mum. Sailor stopped squawking and put his head on one side.

Mrs Brown looked at Sailor, balanced on the cage, his wings still beating and his feathers sticking out at all angles. Then she looked at Nutmeg. 'Don't be naughty, Nutmeg!' she said. 'What are you doing in here?'

'Just playing,' miaowed Nutmeg.

'How did she get in here?' Mrs Brown asked Dan.

'I don't know,' Dan replied.

'You know what we agreed when we first had her,' said Mrs Brown sternly. 'That we'd keep these two apart when none of us was in the room to watch them.'

Dan picked up his kitten. 'I can't believe a tiny thing like you managed to ruffle Sailor's feathers,' he whispered, smiling.

Nutmeg climbed onto his shoulder, right next to his ear. She liked it up there. She could snuggle into the top of his sweater.

'What did you do to poor old Sailor?' Dan asked, stroking her fur all the way down her back to the tip of her soft tail.

'I was only trying to catch him,' Nutmeg purred, trying to look cute.

'She's a sweet little thing,' said Mrs Brown, 'but so naughty!'

'She is only three months old,' said Dan. 'Kittens are supposed to be mischievous at that age.'

Sailor flew across the room and perched on the television. 'Who's a pretty boy, then?' he squawked.

'You are, of course,' said Mrs Brown, feeling in her pocket for a peanut.

Sailor took the nut in his claw and broke open the shell with his beak. 'You're nuts!' he squawked. 'You're nuts!'

Dan laughed. Sailor was always picking up new sayings. 'Come on, Nutmeg,' he said. 'Let's go to my room.'

He walked across the wide hall with Nutmeg balanced on his shoulder, up the stairs and into his bedroom. 'It's a bit quieter in here,' he said.

He put Nutmeg down on the floor then picked up a sock and waved it in front of her. She pounced, but Dan pulled it away just in time. Then he trailed it across the floor for the kitten to chase. It was good fun.

Some time later, Dan left Nutmeg chasing the little ball from his football game while he played on his computer.

'I think I'll explore some more!' miaowed Nutmeg and she climbed up into an open drawer and turned round and round, mixing up all the clothes.

'Don't be naughty, Nutmeg!' sighed Dan. 'Mum will be annoyed if she sees what you've done!'

'Sorry!' miaowed Nutmeg. She jumped down and went over to Dan, leaping on to his lap.

Climbing on to his desk, Nutmeg trod on Dan's computer keyboard.

'Oh, Nutmeg! Now look what you've done,' said Dan, as the game he was playing came to a sudden end. But he wasn't really cross. How could he be cross with such a cute little thing? He lifted Nutmeg gently down on to the floor and began another game.

A few minutes later, Dan realised that Nutmeg had become very quiet. What's she up to now? he wondered. Then he heard a scratching sound and a faint miaow. It didn't take him long to find her. She had crawled into one of the tunnels from his electric car track and was stuck!

'Nutmeg!' he laughed as he gently pulled her free. 'You're the nosiest cat in the world!'

'I know!' miaowed Nutmeg.

Dan watched Nutmeg as she carried on playing. He was really glad he had chosen her out of Bracken's litter of nine very different kittens. Well, she had chosen him really . . . Dan's family had heard about the kittens from Mr Bradman, who was changing the layout of their large garden. He had invited them round to his house to see the litter when they were about four weeks old. Dan hadn't noticed Nutmeg at first. But when he had picked up his coat to get a tissue, he'd found her asleep, up one of his sleeves! She'd crawled in when no one was looking and curled up for a nap.

Three weeks later, when Dan and Mrs Brown had gone back to the Bradmans' to collect Nutmeg, she had scampered towards them, as if she remembered them. And she had settled quickly into her new home.

Dan went back to his computer game and Nutmeg looked around for more places to explore. She spotted that the bedroom door wasn't properly shut. She bounded over to it, pushed her tiny paw into the crack and pulled. It opened further.

She looked back at Dan. He was concentrating hard on his computer, and didn't notice Nutmeg squeezing out of the room.

"What a clever kitten I am!" she miaowed as she ran out on to the landing. She really was getting very good at opening doors. She poked her head through the bars of the banisters at the top of the stairs and looked down into the hall.

It was a very big house and although she had been with the Browns for quite a while now, there were still a few rooms that she hadn't had a chance to explore. Today, she could see that the kitchen door was wide open. She would go in there first.

One step at a time, she bounced down the stairs, then she galloped across the hall and into the kitchen. There was nobody there. 'Good!' she miaowed quietly. 'I can go where I like and do what I want.'

Nutmeg decided to explore some of the kitchen shelves first. Softly, she jumped up and began to prowl along one of the lower ones, smelling each box or bag that she came to.

Everything had a different scent. And some things smelled delicious!

Nutmeg's mouth watered. She reached out her paw and tried to open a few of them, but had no luck, though a few dropped off the shelf and on to the floor.

Then she came to a big blue-and-white striped bag. It was open at the top, but she was too small to see what was in it, so she stood on her hind paws and stretched up, leaning against the bag, trying to see inside.

Suddenly, the bag began to tip and then it toppled over. Loads of powdery white stuff fell out all over the shelf. And all over Nutmeg. Some fell on to the floor and white clouds of it filled the air.

'Aaa . . . tchoo!' sneezed Nutmeg as it went

up her nose. 'Aaa . . . tchoo!'

'There's someone in the kitchen!' she heard Helen call as more and more white stuff got up her nose and made it tickle again.

'Aaa . . . tchoo!' Nutmeg sneezed more flour into the air as Mrs Brown and Helen came into the kitchen. Helen laughed when she saw Nutmeg, but Mrs Brown didn't.

'Oh, Nutmeg – you're so naughty!' cried Mrs Brown.

'I didn't know we had a white kitten,' said Helen, picking up Nutmeg. 'Look at the state of you!'

'I was only having a look round,' miaowed Nutmeg.

Helen stood the kitten on a towel on the kitchen table and began to brush the flour from her fur. Nutmeg wriggled about, trying to escape. Then she caught sight of a bright flash of colour. Sailor was watching from the doorway. But not for long. Mrs Brown quickly went and lifted him up, his claws curling round her hand. 'How did this parrot get out of the sitting-room?' she asked as she carried him away.

'He seems to be following me around,' miaowed Nutmeg. 'He always turns up when I'm having most fun. *And* when I'm being told off!'

2

Mrs Brown came back and began to sweep up the mess. Nutmeg shook herself and sneezed again. Almost all the flour had gone now and Helen let Nutmeg jump down from the kitchen table. She scampered out into the hall in case Helen changed her mind. And there in front of her, the door into Sailor's room was still open!

'You're nuts!' Nutmeg heard as she crept into the room. 'You're nuts!'

Nutmeg took no notice of Sailor. She jumped on to the window sill to see what was happening outside. But as she landed, her paws skidded and she knocked a pottery vase. The vase wobbled, sloshing out water that trickled across the window sill and dripped down on to the carpet. Nutmeg froze, wondering if the vase was going to topple over on to the floor and break. She'd already been in enough trouble for one day.

'You're nuts!' Sailor screeched.

'Be quiet!' Nutmeg hissed back, still watching the vase. But it seemed to have settled and was still again. Phew!

Nutmeg looked at the water on the carpet. There was a dark stain down the wallpaper below the sill, too. She hoped Mrs Brown wouldn't be too cross.

'I'd better get away from here,' she miaowed to herself, 'before anyone sees what I've done.'

'Hello, Sailor!' the parrot squawked, as Nutmeg ran across the room towards the door.

Nutmeg ignored Sailor. He really was too silly, she thought. But as she passed by the table, Nutmeg couldn't resist jumping up to see if there was anything interesting up there.

Sure enough, she found masses of bright, strange-shaped pieces. She'd seen these before. Helen had called it a jigsaw. The pieces seemed to Nutmeg to be asking to be tapped around. She liked the way they skidded across the shiny surface of the polished wood.

Just when she was becoming really skilled at

hitting the pieces a long way, the door opened and Helen came in. 'Nutmeg!' she cried, making a deep frown across her forehead. 'I'd spent ages on that – and now it's ruined!'

'What's the matter?' Mrs Brown called from the kitchen.

'Come and see what Nutmeg's done now!' cried Helen. 'I'll have to do all this again!'

Nutmeg gulped. She could see that Helen was upset. 'I didn't know,' she miaowed. 'I thought anyone could play with your game.'

Mrs Brown rushed into the room. 'Don't be naughty, Nutmeg!' she said loudly when she saw Helen's puzzle.

Nutmeg hung her head. She didn't mean to upset anybody, but she wasn't having a very good day.

'You're nuts!' squawked Sailor, but this time nobody laughed.

Nutmeg leapt at him, but he flew to the safety of the top of his cage again. 'Get off! Get off!' he squawked.

'Don't be naughty, Nutmeg!' Mrs Brown repeated. Then she noticed the wet patch under the window.

'Was this you, Nutmeg?' she sighed, looking for something to mop up the water. 'What are we going to do with you?'

'I don't know,' miaowed Nutmeg. 'But I'll try and be good from now on.'

The family had fish and chips for lunch that day. Nutmeg could smell the delicious fish as soon as Mrs Brown and the children arrived home and unwrapped it in the kitchen. Nutmeg even jumped on the table to get a better look at it. But Mrs Brown lifted her down. 'None for you,' she said.

Dan picked Nutmeg up. 'I'll give you some of mine,' he whispered in her ear. Everyone sat around the dining table to eat. Nutmeg sat under the table, hoping for some odd scraps to fall her way, but she was disappointed.

'You have to wait until we've finished,' whispered Dan.

Sailor watched from a distance. He had been fed already.

'What's for dinner?' he squawked. 'What's for dinner?'

'Fish and chips,' said Dan. 'Hey, shall I teach him to say it?'

'Why not?' said Mrs Brown. 'He likes learning new words.'

Dan finished eating then he took his plate into the kitchen, to put the leftover fish into Nutmeg's dish. Nutmeg sniffed the little white pieces of fish. She had never tasted it before, but her mouth watered and she knew she was going to love it. She nibbled the fish and licked the plate until it was clean. While she ate, she could hear Dan talking to Sailor.

'Fish and chips, Sailor,' he said. 'Come on, say it – fish and chips. Fish and chips. It's easy – fish and chips.'

Nutmeg came back in from the kitchen to watch.

Sailor took a deep breath and closed one eye. Then he lifted his head and opened his beak. 'Chish and fips!' he squawked. 'Chish and fips!'

'No, you silly!' laughed Dan. 'Fish and chips!'

But Sailor seemed to prefer what he had first said. 'Silly Sailor!' he squawked. 'Chish and fips! Chish and fips!'

Everyone was laughing at Sailor, but Nutmeg felt full and rather sleepy. Nobody noticed her creep over and jump up on to the window sill again. She was more careful this time, and didn't knock the vase. She made herself comfortable and fell fast asleep in the sunshine.

Nutmeg woke with a start. She sat up, her heart racing and her bright eyes wide with fright. What had woken her up?

She soon found out: Sailor!

'Chish and fips!' he was squawking. 'Chish and fips!'

Mr Brown was home from work and Dan was getting Sailor to show off his new phrase. Mr Brown was roaring with laughter.

'Well done, Sailor,' he chuckled. 'You're brilliant! And well done, Dan, for teaching him.'

'What's for dinner?' squawked Sailor very loudly. 'Chish and fips!'

Nutmeg had had enough of the parrot's loud voice. She yawned, stood up on the window sill, stretching her back into a high arch, then she jumped nimbly down on to the floor and darted from the room. She crept across the hall and up the stairs, wondering if Helen was in

her room. She would go and see.

Helen was sitting at her dressing table, painting her nails with glittery varnish. She was going out to a school disco later that evening. She saw Nutmeg in the mirror as soon as the kitten entered the room. 'Hello, Mischief,' she said. 'Thought you'd come and disturb me, did you?'

'There's lots in here I haven't discovered yet,' miaowed Nutmeg.

'"I hope you're not going to break anything,' said Helen.

'I'll try not to,' Nutmeg replied.

Suddenly a bell rang, making Nutmeg jump. It was that thing in the hall that they called 'the phone'. The ringing stopped and Nutmeg heard Mr Brown's voice.

'Helen,' Mr Brown shouted. 'Phone!'

'OK, Dad,' called Helen as she leapt up from her dressing table and ran downstairs.

Nutmeg immediately rushed over to the dressing table. She wanted to know what Helen was putting on her fingernails. It was very sparkly. Then something else caught her eye. Helen's hairband was just waiting to be pounced on. But as she pounced, Nutmeg knocked over Helen's sparkly stuff.

She looked at the shiny pool that was growing on the dressing table. 'Uh oh . . .' she mewed, alarmed. She reached out her paw and touched the edge of it. It felt very sticky. Nutmeg sniffed at it, then quickly pulled her nose away. It smelled horrible! It made her feel sick.

Quickly she leapt down, away from the smell. She tried to shake the stuff from her paw, but it had stuck fast.

The wardrobe was open. Nutmeg decided she would explore in there until she felt better.

It was quite dark inside the wardrobe, but Nutmeg could see clearly. There was one of Helen's trainers in the corner, so she jumped into it. She fitted very well, but she soon grew bored with sitting still so she jumped out again. She chewed the shoelace for a while, then pulled at a belt that was hanging from one of Helen's skirts.

Suddenly, Nutmeg froze in terror. Two hollow black eyes were staring at her from a shiny white face. There were red circles on the cheeks and the laughing mouth looked big enough to swallow Nutmeg.

'Help!' she miaowed timidly. But nobody came to rescue her from this frightening creature. 'Stay away!' she hissed.

But the face seemed to loom bigger and bigger. Nutmeg backed away into the far corner of the wardrobe. 'Help!' she miaowed again. But still nobody came. She would have to stay with this terrifying creature forever.

At that moment, Nutmeg heard Helen come back into the room.

'Oh, no!' Helen said. Her voice sounded cross. She must have found the spilled smelly sticky stuff. 'Where's that naughty kitten? Nutmeg! Nutmeg! Where are you?'

'I'm in here,' Nutmeg tried to miaow. But being frightened made her voice very weak. Now she didn't know which was worse, being told off by Helen or being trapped with the frightening creature.

She decided the face was much worse. Helen was sure to forgive her. 'I'm here,' she miaowed a bit louder.

'I can hear you,' called Helen. 'But I can't see you.'

Nutmeg couldn't stand the face any longer. She knew she had to be brave and walk past it. 'Stay away!' she hissed again as she backed slowly towards the wardrobe door. 'Ugly thing, I don't like you,' she hissed. Nutmeg was shaking so much she began to fall over her own paws, but at last she reached the wardrobe door and dashed out, still trembling all over.

Dan was standing in the doorway of Helen's room. He had been in his own room and had heard his sister call out. He looked at Helen, then Nutmeg, then at the pool of sticky nail varnish.

'Don't be naughty, Nutmeg!' he said, but then he noticed her enormous wide eyes and realised that she was shaking. 'She's frightened,' he said, looking angrily at his sister. '"What have you done to her?'

'Nothing!' shouted Helen. 'I came back from the phone and found this! I presumed Nutmeg had done it. That's all. I didn't know she'd gone into the wardrobe.'

Dan went over to Nutmeg and picked her up. He held her close and snuggled her into the neck of his sweater. 'Poor little thing,' he said. 'She's shaking like a leaf.' He stroked Nutmeg gently. 'What's the matter?' he asked her.

Nutmeg looked at the wardrobe. 'T-there's s-something t-terrible in t-there,' Nutmeg miaowed.

3

'I've never seen her like this before,' said Dan. 'Something must have scared her in the wardrobe.'

'In the wardrobe?' said Helen, doubtfully. She opened the wardrobe door wide and peered in. Then she began to laugh. She bent down and pulled something out.

It was the horrible face! Nutmeg disappeared down inside Dan's sweater.

'It's all right, Nutmeg,' said Dan, lifting her out. 'Look! It's only a silly old mask that Helen wore to a fancy dress party the other week.'

Nutmeg looked. Although she still didn't like how it looked, the face wasn't quite so fierce out in the light, cheerful bedroom. And she trusted Dan and believed what he said. Gradually, she stopped shaking. As Helen and Dan stroked her, Nutmeg began to purr.

'Hello, Sailor!' came the sudden squawk from Helen's doorway. Dan and Helen jumped almost as much as Nutmeg did. 'What's for dinner? Chish and fips! Who's a pretty boy, then?'

'Have you escaped from the sitting-room again?' Helen asked the parrot.

'Who's a pretty boy, then?' squawked Sailor. 'Give us a kiss!'

'Not likely!' laughed Helen. 'Anyway, how long have you been there, watching?'

'Clever boy!' squawked Sailor. 'Chish and fips! Chish and fips!'

Nutmeg had heard enough. She leapt out of Dan's arms at Sailor. This time he only just managed to fly out of her reach on to the landing. He sat perched on the banister rail, complaining loudly. 'Get off! Get off! Get off!' he squawked.

'Is Nutmeg being naughty?' Mrs Brown shouted loudly from downstairs. She sounded cross. 'And who let Sailor out of the sitting-room?'

Dan and Helen leaned over the banisters.

'We didn't,' said Dan. 'We were both up here all the time.'

'This is getting ridiculous,' said Mrs Brown. 'We all know he shouldn't be out of there.'

'I reckon he lets himself out,' said Dan.

'Don't be silly,' said Mr Brown who had joined his wife in the hall. 'A parrot couldn't do that.'

'I bet Sailor could!' said Helen. 'He's crafty enough!'

'And Dan, you'll have to find a way to stop that kitten of yours bothering Sailor,' said Mrs Brown.

Dan and Helen laughed. Dan held Nutmeg up next to Sailor.

'Look at the difference in size,' said Dan.

'As if a tiny animal like that could do much harm to a great big bird like Sailor!' said Helen.

Nutmeg purred. 'It won't stop me trying to catch him though. I just love to see his bright feathers ruffled!'

The following day, Dan was getting dressed. He was grinning to himself as he pulled on his sweatshirt. He was thinking about all the mischief Nutmeg had been up to. He tied the laces of his trainers and headed out of his bedroom. Just then, he heard a shout.

'Don't be naughty, Nutmeg!' his mum was screeching.

What on earth has Nutmeg done now? Dan

thought. It must be something really terrible for Mum to make such a fuss!

Dan leapt down the stairs two at a time. As he reached the bottom step he glanced into the kitchen. And there, through the kitchen window he could see his mum! She was in the garden hanging out the washing on the line and talking to Mr Bradman.

Mum moved quickly, Dan thought. And she looks quite calm already. He dashed through the kitchen and out into the garden.

'Hello, Dan,' said Mr Bradman. 'How's that young kitten doing? Still as inquisitive as ever?'

'Yes. Well, actually, that's why I came out,' said Dan. 'I heard Mum shout and I wondered what Nutmeg had done.'

'Me?' said Mrs Brown. 'Shout?'

'Yes,' said Dan.

'When?'

'Just now.'

Mrs Brown smiled and shook her head. 'Not me,' she said. 'I've been out here with Mr Bradman for at least ten minutes, haven't I, Tim?''

Mr Bradman nodded. 'It's true,' he said with a chuckle. 'And not a single shout has passed her lips. You must have imagined it, Dan.'

'No,' said Dan, puzzled. 'I definitely heard it.'

'In fact, I haven't seen Nutmeg this morning,'

said Mrs Brown. 'I thought she must be upstairs with you or Helen.'

Suddenly, they were all shocked to silence.

'Don't be naughty, Nutmeg!' they heard. 'Ha! Ha! Ha! Ha!'

'I told you!' said Dan.

'It certainly sounds like me,' said Mrs Brown. 'What's going on?'

They all ran indoors and met Helen and Mr Brown in the hall.

'Mum!' said Helen. 'What's Nutmeg done?'

Before Mrs Brown could answer, they heard it again.

'Don't be naughty, Nutmeg! Ha! Ha! Ha! Ha!'

The sound was coming from the sitting-room. Dan dashed in, followed by the rest of the family and Mr Bradman.

What they saw made them all laugh. Sailor was flapping around the room with glee, screaming in a perfect imitation of Mrs Brown's voice, 'Don't be naughty, Nutmeg! Ha! Ha! Ha! Ha!'

But where was Nutmeg?

It was Dan who spotted her. She was huddled in the bottom of the huge parrot cage looking very sorry for herself. The cage door was firmly closed.

'Help!' Nutmeg miaowed in a pitiful little voice. 'Let me out. This rotten old bird has locked me in.'

'How did she get in there?' said Helen.

Dan looked at Sailor who seemed very pleased with himself. 'It must have been Sailor,' he said, opening the cage door and reaching in for Nutmeg. 'He must have shut her in.'

Helen laughed.

'Don't be silly, Dan,' said Mr Brown. 'A parrot couldn't do something like that.'

'Yes he could,' said Dan, placing Nutmeg in her favourite place on his shoulder. 'All he had to do was wait until Nutmeg went to explore his cage. She's so nosy, she was bound to go in sometime, weren't you, Nutmeg?'

'Yes,' admitted Nutmeg, mewing pitifully. 'That wily old parrot tricked me!'

'I always knew my parrot was intelligent!' laughed Mrs Brown.

'And I still bet he's the one who's been opening the sitting-room door,' said Dan.

'You're probably right,' said his mum. 'We could test him. Then we'll know what to expect from now on.'

Everyone left the sitting-room and Mr Brown closed the door firmly behind them. They waited in silence in the hall. But not for long! There was a faint scratching sound as the handle on the outside of the door rattled and began to move. A few moments later, Sailor appeared in the doorway.

'Who's a clever boy, then?' he squawked.

'You are!' laughed Mrs Brown. 'More than we realised!'

Mr Bradman went back outside to draw up plans for the garden. The Brown family went back in the sitting-room and sat down in the armchairs.

'It seems we've been blaming Nutmeg for all the mischief around here,' laughed Mr Brown. 'But it looks as if Sailor can be just as naughty!'

'There isn't much point trying to keep them apart any longer,' said Mrs Brown. 'Sailor has certainly proved he can look after himself!'

Nutmeg purred her agreement about that! She snuggled into the top of Dan's sweatshirt, warm and happy now. She loved being part of the Brown family.

'Perhaps you won't be quite so naughty from now on, Nutmeg,' Dan whispered.

Nutmeg rubbed her face against his chin, then looked at Sailor with new respect.

'Or maybe Sailor and I'll get up to mischief together!' she purred. 'That would be great fun!'

And, as Nutmeg watched, Sailor winked his eye.

LUCY DANIELS
Amber

Illustrated by Bill Geldart

*To Hercules, a big cuddly cat, who was loved
right to the tip of his tail*

1

Amber scampered towards the back door. She had heard Mr Bradmans' voice and that meant Lottie, the Bradman's Golden Retriever, would be home from her walk. Amber found Lottie and Mr Bradman in the kitchen.

'I'm glad you're back,' Amber purred happily. Lottie bounded over to Amber and licked the kitten's nose. 'We've had a great walk!' she barked.

Amber looked up at Lottie's friendly face. 'I wish I could have come,' she miaowed. 'Where did you go?'

'Along by the river,' Lottie barked.

'I can see that!' Amber miaowed, looking at Lottie's big soft-padded paws. 'Your paws are all muddy.'

Mr Bradman finished taking off his muddy boots, then grabbed an old towel from under the sink. 'Come on, Lottie,' he said. 'Let's clean you up a bit.'

Lottie went over to Mr Bradman, Amber trotting happily underneath her, running in and out of her legs. Amber knew that Lottie would be careful not to tread on her friend.

Tom was sitting at the kitchen table doing his homework. He laughed. 'Those two are great together, aren't they?' he said. 'And in a funny way they look alike because their coats are such a similar colour.'

'Yes, and you'd think Amber was a puppy not a kitten, the way she behaves!' chuckled Mr Bradman.

'I wish I was!' miaowed Amber.

'Lottie's so good with all the kittens,' said Tom. 'But Amber's definitely her favourite.'

'Of course I am,' purred Amber.

'They'll miss each other when we find Amber a new home,' said Mr Bradman.

'But I don't need a new home,' miaowed Amber. 'I'm very happy here, thank you.'

Mr Bradman began to wipe Lottie's paws with

the towel. Amber pounced on one corner and tugged at it with her claws.

Bracken was sitting in the cat basket in the corner, washing Amber's sister, Clove.

'Don't be a nuisance, dear,' she miaowed at Amber.

'I'm not,' miaowed Amber. 'Lottie loves having me around. But I wish I was allowed to go for a walk with her.'

'Cats don't go for walks,' Bracken miaowed back.

'Why not?' asked Amber.

But Bracken was too busy cleaning behind Clove's ears to answer.

It wasn't fair! Amber thought. Why couldn't a kitten go for a walk? 'In that case, I wish I was a dog!' she miaowed.

'Don't be silly, dear,' miaowed Bracken. 'Anyway, you're too young to be allowed out.'

When Mr Bradman had finished cleaning Lottie, she went to her water bowl to have a drink. Her long floppy tongue lapped the water noisily. Amber ran over and put her front paws on the opposite side of the bowl. Copying Lottie, she lapped away with her tiny tongue.

Tom laughed then got up from the table and reached into a cupboard. 'Watch this, Dad,' he said, fetching out some dog biscuits. 'Here, Lottie,' he called.

Lottie left her water and ran to Tom, her tail wagging furiously. Amber trotted at her heels.

'Lottie, sit,' said Tom. Lottie sat down. Amber sat beside her.

'Good girl, Lottie,' said Tom. 'And good girl, Amber!'

'Woof!' barked Lottie.

'Woof!' miaowed Amber.

'Shake paws,' said Tom. Lottie lifted a front paw and shook Tom's hand. Amber did the same.

'Good girl, Lottie,' said Tom, giving her a dog biscuit. 'Good girl, Amber,' he said, giving her one too.

Amber loved them. They were much more tasty than cat biscuits – and much bigger!

The next morning, when Tom came home from his paper round, he found Lottie gnawing at a large bone with the tiny golden kitten beside her, as usual. Amber's teeth weren't fully grown yet, but she was copying everything that Lottie did.

Lottie stopped chewing when she saw Tom, so Amber stopped, too. And when Lottie ran to greet Tom, Amber was right behind her. Lottie barked and rolled over for Tom to tickle her tummy. Amber did the same.

'Hello, Lottie's little shadow!' Tom laughed and tickled Amber's tummy, too.

'I like that,' purred Amber, rubbing the side of her cheek against Tom's hand.

Mrs Bradman came into the kitchen. She opened some tins and tipped food into several bowls. Then she banged the fork on the side of a tin and Bracken arrived with some of Amber's brothers and sisters.

They went over to the bowls of cat food, but Amber followed Lottie to wait for the dog food bowl.

'Mum,' said Tom, putting the last dish of food

down on the kitchen floor, 'I think I've found someone else who'll have a kitten.'

'Good,' said Mrs Bradman. 'Who?'

Amber pricked up her ears and listened.

'The Green family along the road,' said Tom. 'It's Sam's ninth birthday next week and he's asked for a kitten. They've never had a cat before, only dogs, but they said they'd like to come round tomorrow and choose one. Is that all right?'

'Of course,' said Mrs Bradman.

'They'd better not choose me,' miaowed Amber, with her mouth full, as she moved nearer to Lottie.

The next afternoon after school, Sam Green and his mother arrived at the Bradmans' house. Amber wasn't at all interested – until she noticed that they'd brought three dogs with them!

There was one who looked a little like Lottie, but with a shorter coat. And there was a white one, covered in black spots. And the third one was short – not much taller than Amber – but long and sausage-shaped.

'We thought the dogs ought to come,' said Mrs Green, as they came into the sitting-room. 'There's no point getting a cat that's terrified of dogs.'

'And you'll have to make sure all the dogs are

willing to live with a cat!' said Mrs Bradman.

'Woof!' 'Woof!' 'Woof!' barked the three dogs as soon as they saw Bracken and her kittens. They all bolted upstairs, hissing and spitting as they ran – except Amber.

She stayed beside Lottie who greeted the dogs with interest. They touched noses and walked round each other, sniffing and wagging their tails. Amber tried to do the same.

'That's amazing!' said Mrs Green.

'Wow!' said Sam. 'That kitten isn't afraid at all!'

Amber looked up, surprised. 'Of course I'm not,' she miaowed.

'And she's so sweet!' said Mrs Green, crouching down to get a closer look. 'Have you given her a name?'

'We call her Amber,' said Tom.

'Mmm, it suits her. I think we'd call her that if we chose her,' said Mrs Green.

Sam nodded. 'All the dogs seem to like her,' he said. 'And so do I!' He bent down to stroke the kitten. 'Can we have her?'

'But I live here,' miaowed Amber, scampering away to hide behind Lottie.

A week later, Sam arrived with his father, carrying a large cardboard box with handles on the top.

Amber had almost forgotten about him choosing her. She dashed into the kitchen. Lottie was lying across the mat in front of the boiler.

'Don't tell them I'm here,' Amber miaowed, and she burrowed under one of Lottie's front legs, hoping the Golden Retriever's coat would cover her.

She stayed as still as she could, but her heart was pounding so loudly she was sure everyone would notice her. She listened as Mrs Bradman brought Sam and Mr Green into the kitchen.

Tom and Ellie ran in from the garden.

'Hello,' said Tom. 'Happy Birthday! Have you come for Amber?'

'Yes,' said Sam, fidgeting from one foot to the other. 'I've been dying to come and fetch her all week.'

'She was here a moment ago,' said Mrs Bradman. 'I wonder where she's gone.'

'I've been to the library,' said Sam, as everyone searched for Amber. 'And I borrowed loads of books on kittens. I know all about how to look after one now.'

'That's good,' said Mrs Bradman, peering under the kitchen table. 'I'm glad you're going to look after her so well.'

Not as well as Lottie does, thought Amber.

'And I've had some birthday money,' Sam went

on. 'I went to the pet shop after school today and bought a special cat basket for her and a clockwork mouse and a little ball with a bell in it. Do you think she'll like them?'

'I'm sure she will," said Mrs Bradman.

No I won't! thought Amber. *I've never played with cat toys. Only dog toys!*

"Now where is that kitten?" said Mrs Bradman.

Mr Green bent down to stroke Lottie. 'Hello, you're lovely dog,' he said. Then he began to smile. 'What's this little thing, hidden in your fur?'

'You crafty thing!' Tom laughed as he crouched down and lifted Amber very gently from her hiding place.

'She's very sweet!' said Mr Green.

'I'm sure she'll be very happy with you,' said Mrs Bradman.

'But I want to stay with Lottie,' miaowed Amber.

At that moment, Bracken crept into the room and sat in a corner, well away from Lottie. Tom put Amber down next to her mum for a moment.

'Be good,' said Bracken, licking Amber's nose. 'You're going to be fine with three dogs to follow around!'

Before Amber could reply, Tom had picked

her up again for Ellie and Mrs Bradman to say goodbye.

'Goodbye,' she miaowed pitifully at each of them. Then she looked down at Lottie who was wagging her tail. 'I'll really miss you,' she miaowed.

'And I'll miss you, too, my little friend,' Lottie woofed. 'But you've got some new doggy friends at Sam's house. You won't be lonely. Good luck!'

2

The first thing Amber saw when the box opened a few minutes later was a white face with black spots peering down at her. It was one of the Greens' dogs.

'Remember me?' she miaowed.

'You're Lottie's little friend,' woofed the Dalmatian. 'You've come to live with us, haven't you?'

'Out of the way, Jordan,' Amber heard, as Sam reached into the box and lifted her out. After giving her a quick cuddle he put her down on the carpet.

Amber dashed up to Jordan. 'So are we going

to be friends then?' she miaowed nervously.

Mr Green laughed. 'This one certainly likes dogs!' he said.

Jordan bent down to give Amber a curious sniff. 'Lottie told us you were unusual for a cat,' he woofed.

Amber rubbed the side of her face against Jordan's long, bony legs. 'I like you already,' she purred.

'And you're quite a sweet little thing,' Jordan woofed back.

Amber followed him into the kitchen. Everything looked very different from the Bradmans'. 'Where are the other dogs?' she miaowed.

'In the garden,' woofed Jordan. 'They'll be in soon.'

If the other two are as friendly as Jordan, maybe it won't be too bad here after all! Amber thought to herself.

Sam came into the kitchen, smiling and holding something in his hands. 'Here you are, Amber,' he said. 'A clockwork mouse.' He put the mouse on the floor in front of her.

Amber looked at it. It didn't smell like a mouse. She didn't trust it one little bit, so she began to back away.

Suddenly, the mouse made a strange whirring

noise and started to skim across the kitchen floor. Amber arched her back as the mouse came towards her. 'Get away from me!' she hissed and ran behind Jordan.

'Don't you like it?' asked Sam.

'Get away from me!' Amber hissed again as the mouse came nearer, but at last it slowed down and stopped.

Sam picked it up. 'Oh dear,' he said. 'I bought it specially for you. I thought all cats liked toys like this.'

'Well, I don't,' miaowed Amber. 'I'd rather play with Jordan.'

But Sam didn't seem to understand. 'I've got some more toys,' he said. 'And a basket for you. Let's try that.' He picked Amber up and placed her in the new basket.

Amber didn't feel as comfortable in there as she had in Lottie's basket. It didn't smell right and she didn't want to stay in it.

Just then, she heard a scratching sound on the back door. Sam went to open it and while he wasn't looking, Amber jumped out of the uncomfortable basket.

A Labrador bounded in. 'Hey, Buster!' said Sam.

Buster skidded to a stop and sniffed Amber. 'Remember me?' she miaowed.

'Of course,' barked Buster, and he licked

her nose. It reminded Amber of Lottie and made her feel much more at home.

And then the third dog galloped into the kitchen, yapping loudly. 'Hi, Laddie,' said Sam. 'Come and say hello to the new kitten.'

'Oh, you're here at last!' yapped Laddie, giving her a friendly sniff. Laddie, a small, red Dachshund, was low enough for Amber to sniff back. That made her very happy!

For the rest of the evening, Amber followed the three dogs around. She played with them, ate with them, and that night, she went to sleep curled up with Buster, the Golden Labrador. As she fell asleep under one of Buster's gentle paws, Amber realised she was having too much fun to miss Lottie.

The next morning. Amber woke when Tom pushed the Greens' newspaper through the letterbox. She heard Sam running downstairs to open the front door and scampered into the hall to see her old friend.

'Hello, Amber!' Tom said. 'Have you settled in well?'

'Yes, thanks,' miaowed Amber.

'She's fine,' said Sam, 'thanks to the dogs! But she isn't interested in the cat toys or the new basket I bought her.'

Tom laughed. 'We always said Amber thinks she's a dog!' he said.

Just then, Buster bounded into the hall, took the newspaper in his mouth and ran back into the kitchen to give it to Mr Green. Amber ran after him and returned a few moments later, dragging part of the paper behind her.

'Hey, look at that!' laughed Sam. 'She even wants to carry the paper!'

Tom laughed too.

Amber dropped the bit of newspaper she was carrying. Why were they laughing at her? 'I'll practise,' she miaowed. 'Then you'll see – I can be just like a dog.'

When Tom arrived to deliver the newspaper the next day, Amber was waiting on the mat. She had a piece of paper in her mouth.

Tom peeped through the letterbox and saw her. 'Clever kitten!' he laughed. Amber purred. She liked being praised.

Soon after breakfast, Mrs Green opened the back door and let all three dogs into the garden.

Amber was just about to sneak out with them when Mr Green stopped her. 'No, Amber,' he said. 'You can't go out there yet.' He shut the door firmly.

Amber sat on the mat and looked up at him.

'Why not?' she miaowed.

But Mr Green had hurried away. He was late for work.

Amber jumped up on to the window sill to watch Jordan, Buster and Laddie chasing round the garden. 'Are you having a good game?' she miaowed, but they didn't seem to hear her.

When Sam came downstairs for breakfast, he ran over to Amber and picked her up. He held her gently against his chest. 'You can go out in the garden when you're older,' he said, stroking the back of Amber's head. 'When you've had your injections.'

'Injections?' Amber miaowed.

'All cats have them when they're nine weeks old and twelve weeks old,' Sam went on. 'It's to stop you from getting ill. Your first one's today, at the vet's.'

When Sam lifted Amber into the cardboard cat carrier that afternoon, Amber felt frightened. She didn't know what to expect when she got to the vet's.

But the vet had a kind face and a soft voice. Amber soon forgot her fear. She was so busy looking round the strange new place that she hardly noticed the tiny prick on her neck.

'That wasn't so bad, was it?' the vet said, smiling.

'Oh! Was that it?' miaowed Amber, as Sam placed her back in the cat carrier.

Over the next few weeks, Amber learned to roll over and play dead, chase balls and carry bigger and bigger pieces of paper in her mouth. But she was dying to play out in the garden.

It seemed such a long time, waiting to be twelve weeks old!

At last, Amber had her second injection. And the next day, when the dogs were let out into the garden, Amber was allowed out, too. 'Wait for me!' she miaowed, as they all tumbled out and raced off down the lawn. But the dogs weren't used to having Amber outside with them yet, and they forgot about her at first.

Amber stood by the step and looked around. Now she was in it, the garden seemed enormous! She stepped on to the grass. It was soft and rather wet.

She padded through it, slowly at first. Then she grew braver. She began to run. There was so much to explore!

Soon she was following Buster, Laddie and Jordan as they raced about.

It was the best fun she had ever had!

Later on, when Sam came home from school, he dashed about the garden to play with them. He threw sticks for them to chase. Amber did her best to reach the sticks first, but her tiny legs didn't carry her fast enough.

Sam saw what was happening. He called the dogs to heel, then threw a tiny stick, just for Amber.

Amber streaked after it, picked it up and brought it back to drop at Sam's feet.

'Well done!' he laughed.

'I'm getting more like a dog every day!' Amber miaowed proudly.

She raced off after the dogs, who had gone to see what Mr Green was doing. He had cut a hole in the back door and was fixing a flap over it.

'That's for you, Amber,' he said, showing her how to use it with his hand.

'Try it.'

Cautiously, Amber pushed her nose against the flap. It moved, so that she could walk through the hole, into the kitchen. She turned round and came back out into the garden. 'That's great!' she miaowed. 'Now I can go in and out whenever I want!'

The following morning, Amber saw the dogs sitting by the front door. It was time for Sam to walk to school, and usually, Mrs Green and the dogs kept him company.

Amber got excited. Now that she'd been outside, perhaps she'd be allowed to go too. She went and sat beside them.

'Not you, Amber,' Sam said. 'Cats don't go for walks. Besides,' he smiled, 'we only have three leads!' He clipped them on to the dogs' collars.

After they had left, Amber walked miserably into the sitting-room and leapt on to an armchair. She'd have a snooze while they were out, she decided. The only good thing about being a cat was being allowed to sleep on the furniture! That was something the dogs weren't allowed to do!

But then Amber remembered her new cat flap.

I could sneak out and follow them! she thought excitedly.

Amber leapt out of the chair and ran into the kitchen. She pushed her way through the cat flap and sped down the back garden. She could hear Laddie yapping to the other two as usual, and followed the noise.

Climbing over the garden fence, Amber raced through an alley that led out on to Liberty Street. She was just in time to see Mrs Green, Sam and the dogs turning the corner.

Amber raced on after them. What an adventure! She had never gone further than the garden before. Her heart was racing with excitement, but she felt nervous, too. There were so many different sounds and smells.

Keeping close to the hedges and walls, Amber followed the dogs along Liberty Street and round the corner into a busier road. The noise of the traffic and the bustle of so many people almost made her turn back. *But if I want to be a dog, I'll have to act like one*, she thought. *Buster, Jordan and Laddie are brave and so am I!*

Mrs Green and Sam came to a part of the road that was striped. Amber watched them stop, then walk across the stripes to get to the other side. She was just about to follow when she heard her name.

'Amber? It is Amber, isn't it?'

Amber looked up at the lady who had spoken to her. It was Tom Bradman's gran, Mrs Jennings, wearing her big white coat. Mrs Jennings was a lollipop lady. She stopped the traffic with a big stick, so children on their way to school could cross the road.

'Yes,' miaowed Amber. 'Only I'm trying to be a dog.'

'You shouldn't be out on your own,' said Mrs Jennings. She looked across the road at Sam and Mrs Green.

'I'm trying to catch them up,' miaowed Amber. 'So I can go for a walk with them.'

'Mrs Green!' called Mrs Jennings. 'Sam!'

Mrs Green and Sam turned round and saw Amber. 'Oh no!' Amber heard Sam shout worriedly. 'Amber shouldn't be here, by the main road – it's dangerous!'

'I'll take her home if you like,' called Mrs Jennings. 'I finish here in a couple of minutes.'

'Thanks,' called Mrs Green. 'I'd be very grateful. My husband's at home to answer the door.'

But Amber wanted to do things by herself. So before Mrs Jennings could pick her up, Amber darted away, back along the busy road to Liberty Street.

A black kitten appeared from the shop on the corner. It was Jet, Amber's brother.

'Hello, Jet,' Amber miaowed. 'Do you live here, then?'

'Yes,' miaowed Jet. 'What have you been doing?'

'I was trying to be a dog and go for a walk,' miaowed Amber. 'But I didn't get very far. I'm on my way home.'

A shadow-grey kitten padded down from some steps nearby and came to join in the conversation. It was their sister, Emerald, who also lived in Liberty Street.

'Hello, Emerald,' miaowed Amber. She was really pleased to see her brother and sister. But before they could talk any more, Amber saw Mrs Jennings coming along to look for her. Not wanting to get into more trouble, she ran off home.

3

A few minutes later, Amber sat in Laddie's box feeling very sorry for herself. After speaking with Mrs Jennings, Mrs Green had firmly locked the cat flap.

'I hate being a cat!' Amber mewed. 'Why can't I be a dog?' She thought about Jet and Emerald. They seemed to like being cats. Amber couldn't imagine why.

The cat flap stayed locked the next time her friends went out for a walk. And the next time. In fact the Greens seemed determined to stop her going with them. Amber felt really fed up. *Will I ever be able to go for a walk, like a dog?* she wondered.

Her chance came sooner than she expected. One Saturday afternoon, the Greens forgot to lock the cat flap. Amber waited for them to leave, then she ran straight through the cat flap, over the garden fence and down the alley into Liberty Street.

The Greens weren't walking towards Sam's school this time – they were going the other way. Amber followed them, staying hidden by jumping from garden to garden down the street.

Soon they came to the edge of town. All Amber could see ahead was open green space. *Wow!* she thought.

Sam let the dogs off their leads and they bounded off. This open countryside was a new experience for Amber and her heart beat fast. She wanted to stop and sniff at everything and explore this new place. But more than that, she wanted to play in all this space with Buster, Jordan and Laddie.

Suddenly she heard Laddie bark and he came running towards her, followed by Buster and Jordan. The three dogs ran rings round Amber, barking loudly.

'Shh!' miaowed Amber. 'Don't let them know I'm here.'

But it was too late. Sam came running over. 'What have you found?' he called to the dogs. 'A rabbit?'

He stopped and stared. 'Oh, no!" he cried. 'Mum, Dad! Who forgot to lock the cat flap?'

'We'll have to go back,' said Mrs Green when she saw the naughty kitten.

Mr Green nodded. 'We can't have her following us any further.'

'Why not?' miaowed Amber. 'I'm not any trouble.'

'Why not?' asked Sam. 'She does everything else that dogs do, so why can't she come for a walk?'

'Thanks, Sam!' miaowed Amber. 'That's what I've been waiting to hear!'

Mrs Green laughed. 'Oh, all right,' she said. 'If that cat's so determined to be a dog!'

Amber was glad she didn't have to stay hidden any more. It was wonderful to race through the fields with her three friends. But when they came to a farmyard Sam picked her up. 'We have to walk more slowly through here,' he said. 'So we don't frighten the animals.'

Mr and Mrs Green kept Buster, Jordan and Laddie on their leads until they came to open fields again. Then Sam put Amber down to run with the dogs again.

All of a sudden, Amber heard a snort. What's that? She turned to look and froze with surprise. An enormous brown animal was staring fiercely at them all. It had wild brown eyes, a big ring through its nose and two very sharp-looking horns!

Mrs Green screamed.

'A bull!' shouted Mr Green. 'Run!'

'What's a bull?' Amber miaowed. But everyone had started running. Mr Green led the way across the field, pulling Mrs Green by the hand. Mrs Green had grabbed Sam and was dragging him along behind her. The dogs bounded speedily ahead of them towards the gate at the side of the field.

'Come on, Amber,' Sam shouted over his shoulder.

But the bull had rounded on Amber and stood in her way. 'You don't seem very friendly,' she miaowed nervously.

'I'm not!' roared the bull.

Amber began to tremble. 'Help!' she mewed. Then, out of the corner of her eye, she noticed a tree nearby. *I can climb that!* she thought. The bull took his eyes off her to watch the others, as they climbed the fence to safety. Amber took her chance. She streaked away from him and began to haul herself up the tree, faster than she'd ever climbed before. *Quick, quick,* she said to herself, as she dug her claws into the bark.

Amber was halfway up the trunk when the bull turned back and saw she was gone. With a roar

that echoed through the branches, he lost interest and lumbered off to the other end of the field.

Thank goodness I'm a cat! Amber thought for the first time ever. *Dogs can't climb trees!*

Checking that the bull wasn't looking, Amber jumped down from the tree. Then making herself as low as possible to the ground, she scuttled across the field to the fence, and joined the others. 'Hello!' she miaowed.

'Amber!' Sam cried. 'You're safe!'

'I thought the bull must have got you!' barked Jordan.

'It's a good job cats can climb trees!' said Mrs Green. 'That must have saved your life, Amber!'

'I know!' miaowed Amber.

'Come on,' said Mr Green. 'Let's go home.'

They had almost reached their house in Liberty Street when a black kitten jumped down from a wall in front of them. Amber heard Mrs Green gasp.

'Oh! It made me jump!' she said. 'My nerves are shattered by that bull!'

But Amber knew who it was. 'Hello, Jet,' she miaowed. 'We've just had a great adventure.'

'So you managed to go on your walk!' miaowed Jet.

The kittens touched noses and Amber told Jet about the bull and how she had climbed the tree to escape from it.

'Well done,' purred Jet. 'Now perhaps you'll agree that being a cat is best!'

'Mmm,' Amber miaowed. 'Maybe you're right!'

LUCY DANIELS
Weed

Illustrated by Bill Geldart

For Figaro and Mist

1

Weed, the tiniest of Bracken's kittens, was snoozing beside her mum. She felt warm breath on her face and opened one eye. A strange-looking woman was staring down at her with big brown eyes, ringed in black. Her mouth was a rather scary bright red.

I don't like the look of her! Weed decided. She squeezed both eyes shut and wriggled closer to Bracken, hoping the woman would go away.

Weed was the last of Bracken's litter to be born, and a small, scraggy, quiet little thing. Now she was the only kitten left in the basket in the Bradmans' kitchen in Liberty Street. All her brothers and sisters had found new homes.

'Let's have a look at you then!'

Suddenly Weed felt a bony hand with long sharp nails yank her away from the safety and warmth of her mum. She felt herself being whooshed through the air and opened her eyes wide in fright. She was being held by the scary woman!

The familiar, cosy scent of Bracken was replaced by the overpowering smell of the woman's strong perfume. 'Oh, I can't breathe,' Weed spluttered. 'Atishoo!'

'Oh, yuk!' The woman's red mouth twisted in horror as Weed sneezed in her face. She let go of the kitten.

Weed felt herself falling through the air. 'Help!' she miaowed.

A pair of large warm hands caught her. Phew! Then she felt herself being lifted upwards again. Weed turned her head to see who was holding her now. It was a man, with smiling blue eyes. 'Let's have a look at you then,' he said in a deep voice. Weed blinked up at him. He didn't seem so bad, she thought.

The man cupped her in one hand and with the other picked up a white stick that was glowing at one end. He sucked on it, then breathed out a puff of white smelly smoke all over Weed. She coughed and spluttered, 'Oh no, I really can't breathe now!'

The man hurriedly tried to pass Weed to a girl that was standing next to the scary woman. But the girl held her hands away.

'No, I don't want to hold her,' she said, sulkily. 'I don't want that kitten – I want a really pretty one.'

The man sighed and put Weed back down in the basket, next to Bracken.

Phew! Weed thought. *What a relief! I'd much rather stay here with the Bradmans.* She huddled as close as she could to her mum, curled into a tight ball in the basket and closed her eyes.

'Sorry. Your kitten isn't exactly what we're looking for,' said the man, puffing on his cigarette as he followed his wife and daughter out of the room.

As Mrs Bradman saw the family out, the girl was saying, 'I don't want a kitten like that. I want a really pretty one . . .'

'Thank goodness they've gone,' Tom Bradman said as the front door was shut. 'They didn't seem very nice.'

'Poor Weed,' said Ellie, looking at Weed, snuggled up next to Bracken. 'What are we going to do with you?'

When people had come to choose one of

Bracken's kittens they'd chosen their kitten for its lovely coat, or pretty face or cheeky personality. But Weed didn't have any of these attractions. And so far, no one had wanted her.

'Don't worry, someone, somewhere will want her,' said Mrs Jennings, Ellie's gran. Mrs Jennings lived just down the road in a garden flat and was always popping in and out of the Bradman house. She'd been there when Bracken had given birth to her nine kittens and had always had a soft spot for little Weed. She was also the local lollipop lady.

Hearing Mrs Jennings's voice, Weed opened her eyes. She loved Gran. 'I wish you wanted me,' she mewed.

'I hope you're right, Gran,' said Ellie, frowning. 'But we have to make sure Weed goes to exactly the right kind of home. We can't let her go just anywhere, to get rid of her.'

'Of course not,' Mrs Bradman said, putting an arm round her daughter. 'You know we'd never do that.'

All the Bradmans were worried that Weed wouldn't find another home. But Weed wasn't worried at all. She didn't mind how long she stayed with the Bradmans. The longer the better, as far as she was concerned! Now that her brothers and sisters had moved away she got to be close to her mum all day long and had loads of attention from the Bradmans.

The doorbell rang.

'That'll be the Taylors,' Mrs Bradman said. 'They sounded really nice on the telephone.' Gran went with her to the door to meet them.

A few moments later, three children pushed their way into the kitchen. They all raced towards the cat basket.

'I'm going to see the kitten first,' one of the boys said.

'But I'm going to hold her first,' said the other.

'No, I am!' shrieked the girl. 'Mum said I could be first!'

Oh no, am I going to be pulled to bits now? Weed wondered, looking up at the squabbling children. She tried to wriggle under Bracken, but three pairs of hands reached out for her at once and she didn't have a chance. They pushed and pulled the basket, each trying to grab hold of Weed. Bracken yowled in alarm.

'I've got her,' the older boy shouted.

'No, you haven't. I've got her,' said the other.

'But I'm supposed to be holding her,' the girl screeched. 'Give her to me!'

For a few seconds Weed was crushed against a woolly blue sweater. Then her face was squashed into a red anorak. And after a while a

pair of sticky hands held her against a white cotton sweatshirt.

'I can't see what she looks like,' the girl wailed.

'Let go and I'll show you,' the older boy shouted.

'No, you let go and I'll show you both,' the younger boy screamed.

'Put me back. Please put me back,' Weed miaowed, squirming to get free. She caught sight of a horrified Ellie and Tom, then a man and woman came into the kitchen.

Mrs Bradman and Gran followed them in. 'Oh, my goodness!' they cried, as they saw the Taylor children grabbing Weed – in between punching, slapping and pulling one another's hair!

'Daniel, Sam, Kate!' said Mrs Taylor in a high, agitated voice. 'Do calm down!' she pleaded.

'Mum! You said I could be first!' Kate cried, red in the face.

'No, you said I could,' the older boy complained.

'It's my turn, Mum!' the younger boy whined.

'Leave the children to sort it out for themselves,' said the rather sour-faced Mr Taylor to his wife.

Just then, Mr Bradman, who had been digging the garden, hurried into the kitchen to see what was going on. He had heard the commotion through the open kitchen window.

Lottie, the Bradmans' dog, bounded in after him, barking. She rushed up to the biggest boy who was clutching Weed, and pulled at his anorak.

'Hey, let go of my kid, you vicious dog!' Mr Taylor shouted. He swung a foot to kick out at Lottie. The Golden Retriever managed to dodge the blow and carried on barking loudly.

Mr Bradman had seen enough. 'I think it's time we put the kitten back with her mother, don't you?' he told the Taylor children calmly but firmly. And he quickly lifted Weed out of the older boy's hands and set her back beside Bracken.

Then he turned to Mr and Mrs Taylor. 'I'm afraid there's been a mistake,' he said. 'Weed isn't in need of a new home after all.' He ushered them out of the kitchen and towards the front door.

'Well, that was a waste of time, wasn't it,' Mr Taylor snapped angrily at his wife.

'Let's just go!' she snapped back.

'Mum, you said we were getting a new kitten,' the older boy whined.

'You promised we'd get one today,' his younger brother joined in.

'I want that kitten – and I want it now!' Kate squealed as the front door banged shut behind them.

Back in her basket Weed was shivering with fright. 'Oh, that was awful,' she mewed, as Bracken gently licked her to try and calm her down.

'There's no way we could ever let Weed go to a difficult family like that,' Mrs Bradman said. 'They really upset her.' She shook her head. 'And Mrs Taylor sounded so nice and polite on the phone! What a shock to find out what they were really like!'

Gran went over to the cat basket and bent down to stroke Weed.

'They almost pulled me apart,' Weed mewed up at her.

'There, there, little one,' Gran whispered softly. 'Don't you worry. Gran won't let you go to a new home unless it's absolutely perfect.'

'I wish I didn't have to go anywhere at all,' Weed miaowed back.

2

Later that evening, when Gran had gone home and the Bradmans were chatting in the kitchen, the doorbell rang.

'I'll get it,' Tom said, leaping up to open the door.

'I'm Mrs Jones and this is my daughter Alice,' a woman's voice said. 'We heard that you were looking for a home for a kitten and we'd love to see it. I hope you don't mind us dropping round like this. Can we come in now?'

'I think so,' Tom said. Then he shouted through to the kitchen, 'There are some people here to see Weed. Is it all right if I bring them in?'

'That's fine,' Mrs Bradman replied and she hurried out to meet them.

Weed looked up from the basket. She felt anxious. *I don't want any more people staring and holding me,* she thought, unhappily.

She could hear voices and footsteps coming down the hall. Just before Tom and Mrs Bradman and the visitors came into the kitchen, Weed skipped out of her basket and ran through the arch to the adjoining sitting-room. Flattening her tummy against the floor, she crawled under the sofa.

Bracken saw her go and so did Ellie. But neither of them did anything to stop her. Mr Bradman, who was busily folding up the newspaper he'd been reading, hadn't noticed.

'This is Weed,' Tom said, leading Alice Jones towards the basket. Then he stopped, surprised. 'Oh! She was here a minute ago. Did anyone see where Weed went?' he asked.

Ellie shook her head, keeping her fingers crossed behind her back.

'She can't have gone far,' Mr Bradman said.

Tom and his mum and dad began to walk around the room, calling Weed. Ellie joined in, not wanting to give the game away. "Come here, Weed,' she called. 'There's someone here to see you.'

But I don't know if I want to see them, Weed thought, staying where she was, in her hiding place under the sofa. She could hear everything that was going on in the kitchen.

'I can't wait to see this kitten,' Alice said excitedly. 'I hope we can find her soon. I'm longing to hold her.'

'Alice has been wanting a kitten for ages,' Mrs Jones explained.

Alice sounds quite nice, Weed thought, slithering forward far enough to peep out from her hiding place and take a look at the visitors.

First she saw the back of Alice's white trainers and green tracksuit bottoms. Looking up, she saw that Alice had long brown hair. Then Alice turned round and Weed saw her friendly face.

She looks really nice, Weed thought. Almost as nice as Ellie. She crawled back under the sofa to think. *If I really do have to go, perhaps it might be all right to go and live with a girl like her.*

Meanwhile, Mr Bradman and Tom began searching the sitting-room.

'Weed, where are you?' Mr Bradman called. 'There's nothing to be frightened of.'

Weed wasn't quite sure yet and stayed where she was.

Mr Bradman lifted up the cushions on the sofa and looked under the piles of newspapers and magazines that littered the room.

Tom opened and shut cupboard doors. 'Come on, Weed. Everything's OK. Come on out," he called.

Ellie came into the room and, on her hands and knees, looked under the sofa. 'Weed, I think you might like Alice. Perhaps you should come and meet her,' she whispered.

Weed crept a little closer. *If everyone thinks Alice is OK, then perhaps I should trust them*, she thought. 'Maybe you're right,' she mewed in her tiniest voice.

She had just decided to crawl out to take a proper look at Alice when Mrs Bradman asked, 'Have you have got any other pets, Alice?'

'Yes,' Alice replied, grinning. 'I've got loads.'

'Oh,' Ellie said, going back into the kitchen. 'How many?'

Weed watched Alice hold up her fingers and begin to count. 'I've got two hamsters and three guinea pigs, four rabbits and two bantam hens that lay eggs. Then I've got a pet snake and some fish and I've got a lovely cuddly chinchilla that hops about all over the place . . .'

As Alice listed all her pets, the Bradmans all stopped looking for Weed. Lottie, who had been about to leap forward and sniff around the sofa so that they would know where Weed was hiding, backed away and sat in her corner by the door.

Meanwhile, Weed crept right back under the sofa. *I don't want to live with lots of other pets*, she thought worriedly. *I might not like them and they might not like me!*

'That's all of them,' Alice said. 'But I don't have a kitten and I'm simply longing for one.'

'Well, I'm afraid we seem to have lost our kitten,' said Mrs Bradman. She looked at Mrs Jones. 'I'm so sorry . . . Um . . . we'll give you a ring when we find her.'

A couple of minutes later, Weed heard the front door close and Mrs Bradman came back into the kitchen. 'With all those other pets to look after, Alice wouldn't have much time for Weed,' she said.

Mr Bradman nodded. 'It's a pity because she's a nice little girl,' he said, sitting back down at the kitchen table.

'Yes, but Weed deserves someone who has plenty of time to give her lots of love and attention,' Ellie said fiercely.

Now that it was safe again, Weed crawled out from under the sofa and scuttled into the kitchen.

'So there you are,' said Tom. 'Where have you been hiding?'

Weed rubbed up against Ellie's legs. 'Thank you for helping me,' she miaowed. Then she scampered over to the basket and happily snuggled up beside Bracken.

Several days passed. Nobody phoned about a kitten and nobody came to the door looking for one.

'Do you think we should put up some notices?' Tom suggested one morning at breakfast. 'I could ask Angie and Steve if I could put one up in their shop window.' Tom was a paperboy. Early every morning, he delivered newspapers for the shop on the corner of Liberty Street. It was run by Angie and Steve, who had given a home to Jet, another of Bracken's kittens.

'Maybe,' said Mr Bradman, sipping his tea. 'But it seems as though everyone who wants a kitten round here has already got one.'

Ellie was buttering her toast. She listened, but didn't join in the conversation. She had grown more and more fond of Bracken's last little kitten. She dreaded the day when she would have to say goodbye to her.

Ellie was still thinking of Weed as she walked to school.

As always, Gran was standing at the zebra crossing in her big white coat. She held up her lollipop-shaped sign to stop the traffic while children crossed the road. As she walked back to the pavement, she noticed Ellie.

'Morning, love,' she said, giving her a hug. 'You look very glum! What's the matter?'

'It's Weed, Gran,' Ellie sighed.

'Oh, have you found a home for her then?' her gran asked, looking a little bit upset.

'No, that's the problem,' said Ellie. 'Mind you, I don't really want her to go at all.'

Her gran smiled. 'Neither do I,' she confided.

'But there haven't been that many people interested in Weed,' Ellie said, standing on one foot and then the other. 'I'm scared that we'll have to give Weed to someone who's not quite right.' She looked at her gran. 'Can't you think of anyone who would make a good owner for our Weed, Gran?'

'Not off the top of my head,' said Gran. 'But I'll try.'

That afternoon, as Ellie was coming in from school, the telephone rang. Ellie picked it up. It was a Mr Clarke. 'I've heard you've got a kitten that needs a home,' he said in a friendly voice. 'And she sounds just right for my nephews.'

'Could you bring them round to meet her?' Ellie asked.

'I don't think that's necessary,' Mr Clarke replied. '*I* can decide if she's right for the boys.'

Ellie wasn't happy about that. She called her

mum to the phone and was relieved when she heard her firmly telling Mr Clarke, 'But we have to see if the boys are right for our kitten.'

Reluctantly, Mr Clarke agreed to call round that evening with the boys. But when the doorbell rang at seven o'clock, he stood alone on the doorstep.

'Oh, where are your nephews?' Ellie asked in surprise, when she opened the door.

'I'm afraid they were busy tonight,' he explained. 'But I thought I'd come by anyway as you were expecting me. I'd love to see the kitten.'

Ellie showed Mr Clarke into the kitchen.

He went across to Bracken's basket and picked Weed up. 'What a tiny little thing you are,' he said, smiling.

Weed sat in the palms of his large hands and looked up at his friendly round face and warm brown eyes. She felt safe in his big, strong hands and didn't struggle or try to jump back into her basket. *Perhaps you're not too bad,* she thought.

Mr and Mrs Bradman were surprised and pleased. Tom grinned and Ellie, who had been pacing up and down since Mr Clarke had phoned, began to relax.

'Why don't you join us for a cup of tea?' Mrs Bradman suggested. 'And tell us about your nephews.'

Mr Clarke sat at the table with Weed on his lap, describing the boys. 'Simon and Jake are seven and eight years old and they're lively young lads,' he said. 'With lots of energy.'

'Have they got any other pets?' Ellie asked, passing him the milk.

'Thanks. No, but they've been wanting one for a long time. They'd love a little kitten like this.' Mr Clarke helped himself to the sugar and stirred his tea. He looked down at Weed who was licking his hand.

'If the boys are like you,' Weed miaowed, 'I suppose I wouldn't mind living with them.'

Mr and Mrs Bradman continued to chat to Mr

Clarke. Everyone was smiling and beginning to feel that perhaps they'd found the right home for Weed at last. Mr Clarke sipped his tea and stroked Weed affectionately.

Then Mrs Bradman said, 'Of course, we would still have to meet the boys and their parents before we could let Weed go.'

'But I really wanted the kitten as a surprise,' Mr Clarke said, looking disappointed. Then he sighed. 'To tell you the truth,' he said, 'the boys have been getting into a little bit of trouble lately. I thought having a kitten might help to calm them down – stop them being so rough—'

'What kind of trouble?' Mr Bradman asked seriously.

'Well, they smashed a window – and they threw stones at the neighbour's dog,' Mr Clarke admitted, looking embarrassed.

Over in the cat basket Bracken's fur began to stand on end. Lottie, who had been dozing on her blanket, pricked up her ears and growled.

Ellie stared in disbelief at Mr Clarke and shook her head vigorously at her mother. *What if Mr Clarke was wrong? What if having a kitten didn't calm his nephews down – and they were cruel to sweet little Weed? No! They couldn't risk it!*

Weed hadn't liked what she'd heard either. She looked across at Bracken and began to mew. "I think he's all right – but I don't like the sound of his nephews!'

Just then the telephone rang and Ellie ran into the hall to answer it. A few moments later, she let out a happy shriek. Then she called Mrs Bradman to the phone.

Everyone in the kitchen stood around, looking uncomfortable. Then Mrs Bradman and Ellie came back in. Ellie was smiling widely.

'I'm afraid there's been a change of plan, Mr Clarke,' Mrs Bradman said. 'Someone else, already interested in Weed, is going to give her a home.'

3

'Well, that's a shame,' said Mr Clarke, looking disappointed. He put Weed back down in the cat basket next to Bracken, who pulled her kitten close and began to give her a wash.

'Thank goodness!' Bracken purred. 'I didn't want you to go and live with those two cruel boys, either!'

'I suppose I'll have to think of something else to keep those two young rascals out of mischief,' Mr Clarke continued.

'I think that would be best,' replied Mr Bradman.

Mr Clarke finished his tea and let Mrs Bradman show him out.

'Well done, Mum,' said Tom, as she came back into the kitchen. 'That was a clever excuse.'

'It's not a excuse – it's true!' Ellie said, happily. She went over and picked Weed up, cuddling the kitten against her chest. 'Someone does want you, little Weed.'

'Who?' asked Tom and Mr Bradman, surprised.

'Yes, who?' Weed miaowed.

Ellie smiled at her mum, who smiled back at her. 'We're not telling, just yet,' she said mysteriously. 'Just wait and see.'

'But why do we have to wait?' Tom asked. 'It's not fair. Come on, Ellie, tell us.'

'You'll find out tomorrow night,' his sister replied. 'Promise!'

That evening Weed curled up close beside Bracken in the cat basket. *Is this really the last evening I'll spend here?* she wondered.

She looked around the Bradmans' untidy kitchen and remembered all the times she'd spent there. First there was the crowded basket with all her noisy brothers and sisters fighting to get close to their mum. Then, one by one, the other kittens had left for their new homes – until she was the only one left. Since then, Weed had enjoyed having a special time, with Bracken all to herself, and lots of attention from the Bradman family and

Lottie, their dog. *But where am I going to now?* she wondered. *Which home has Ellie decided is right for me?*

Weed thought long and hard about all the people who had been to see her. None of them seemed right to her. *Well, it can't be the Walkers, because they didn't want me,* she decided. *And surely it's not the Taylors who were so angry with each other they almost pulled me apart? And it can't be Alice because everyone said she had too many pets already . . . So who can it be?*

Weed stretched and yawned. She was too tired to think about it any more. She snuggled into Bracken's fur and closed her eyes for her last precious night's sleep beside her mum.

The next day, before Tom left for his paper round, he dashed across to say goodbye to Weed as he did every morning. But this time he lifted her right out of the basket and gave her a kiss on the nose. 'It's not going to be the same without you,' he whispered. 'I'm really going to miss your sweet little face.'

'I'm going to miss you too,' Weed miaowed.

After Tom had gone, Lottie bounded over and asked Weed if she wanted to go and play in the garden. Since it had taken such a long time to find Weed a new home, she'd had her injections and for the last couple of weeks had been allowed to go outside.

'Oh, yes please!' Weed miaowed, thinking it would help to take her mind off things. She wriggled out through the cat flap and scampered across the grass.

Then she hid behind a bush and waited for the Golden Retriever to bark for someone to open the back door.

It didn't take Lottie long to find Weed, once Ellie had opened the back door for her. She chased Weed through the flowerbeds, yapping gently at her back legs.

Weed let Lottie catch her up and they both collapsed on the grass, panting.

'Who am I going to play with in the garden when you've gone?' Lottie barked. 'Your mum has never really liked playing with me.'

'I don't know,' mewed Weed sadly, reaching over to lick her friend's nose.

When Weed climbed back through the cat flap, Mr Bradman was just leaving for work. She twined round his legs, purring.

Mr Bradman stroked the top of Weed's head. 'The house is going to feel a bit empty without you, little one,' he said sadly. 'You've been with us so long, we've all got used to having you here.'

But Ellie was cheerful as she left for school. 'See you later, Weed,' she called over her shoulder. 'And don't worry – everything's going to be all right.'

'I wish you'd tell me where I'm going,' Weed miaowed. But Ellie just grinned at her mum and left.

'Hello, Gran,' said Tom as he opened the door that evening. Gran always came round to dinner on a Tuesday. 'Did you hear about Weed? She's got a new owner – but Mum and Ellie won't tell us who it is yet!'

'Is that right?' said Gran, giving her Tom a kiss. 'I'm sure we'll find out soon enough,' she said, then followed Tom into the kitchen.

Everyone sat at the kitchen table as Mrs Bradman served up a big bowl of pasta.

'OK. Now I'm going to tell you about Weed's new home,' Ellie said, grinning. She took a deep breath and looked around the table.

Everyone waited expectantly. Lottie moved closer and put her head on one side to listen and Bracken sat up in her basket. Weed stopped washing herself. *Here goes*, she thought, swivelling her ears forward so she wouldn't miss anything.

'Well,' Ellie began. 'Weed's new home is really close to here and there aren't any other pets. It's got a nice garden and a very loving owner, who says that Weed can come home and visit Bracken and all of us whenever she wants to.'

'That sounds good,' Weed miaowed. Bracken purred and gave her a motherly lick. Lottie barked her approval, too.

'That sounds great,' Mr Bradman said. 'But where exactly is it?'

'And how can you be so sure it's right for Weed?' Tom added insistently.

'And who is it?' Weed miaowed.

'I know it's right, because I know Weed's new home very well,' Ellie explained. 'We all do!' she

laughed. 'And we all know the owner as well as anyone in our family.'

'That's impossible!' Tom exploded.

'It isn't,' Gran interrupted. 'Because . . . it's me!'

'That's why I didn't tell you yesterday,' Ellie continued. 'Because I wanted Gran to be here, too.'

But nobody was listening to Ellie any more. The whole table had erupted as they all jumped up to give Gran a hug and a kiss.

'Hurrah!' shouted Tom.

'Fantastic!' said Mr Bradman, clapping his hands. 'I can't believe the answer was right under our noses all the time.'

Thoroughly excited by the celebrations, Lottie barked and jumped up at everyone to join in. Bracken jumped out of her basket, miaowing loudly. As for Weed, she trembled with excitement. Then she skipped out of the basket after her mum, and skidded across to Gran.

Everyone looked down at the little kitten.

'How do you feel about coming to live with me then, little one?' Gran said. She reached out a hand and tickled Weed under the chin.

Purring with happiness, Weed jumped up on to Gran's lap. She looked up at her new owner's kind, friendly face. 'The only place I would ever really want to live, other than here,' she miaowed, 'is down the road with you!'

FROG FRIENDS
Animal Ark Pets 15

Lucy Daniels

The frogs that come to Farmer Jessop's pond every spring to lay their spawn have turned up to find it has been filled in! Another pond must be found for the frogs if their tadpoles are to survive. Mandy suggests that the school pond would make a perfect new home. But will the frogs agree?

BUNNY BONANZA
Animal Ark Pets 16

Lucy Daniels

Mandy and James are keen to take part in a national fundraising event for animals. But how? Then James has a brainwave: a gathering of pet rabbits. Owners can pay to join in! But will there be enough rabbits to make it a bunny bonanza?

FERRET FUN
Animal Ark Pets 17

Lucy Daniels

Freddie, a stray ferret, is found under the shed at Lilac Cottage. To make Freddie feel at home, Mandy comes up with a way to include her in a school Fun Day to raise money for new story books. But then Freddie goes missing. Will she turn up in time for the ferret fun?

RAT RIDDLE
Animal Ark Pets 18

Lucy Daniels

Mandy and James's schoolfriend Martin has been given a pair of fancy rats for his birthday. Cheddar and Pickle love to race around their incredible 'Rat Run'. At first Mandy finds that Pickle is the fastest. But then Pickle's times begin to slow down. Could something be wrong?

FOAL FROLICS
Animal Ark Pets Summer Special

Lucy Daniels

Mandy and James are on holiday with Mandy's family. All sorts of things are disappearing from the campsite, and now golf balls from the nearby golf course are going missing too. It's a mystery until Mandy and James catch the thief red-handed: a cheeky foal called Mischief! The bad-tempered groundsman at the golf course wants Mischief removed. Can Mandy and James find a way for the foal to stay?

LUCY DANIELS
Animal Ark Pets

0 340 67283 8	Puppy Puzzle	£3.50	❐
0 340 67284 6	Kitten Crowd	£3.50	❐
0 340 67285 4	Rabbit Race	£3.50	❐
0 340 67286 2	Hamster Hotel	£3.50	❐
0 340 68729 0	Mouse Magic	£3.50	❐
0 340 68730 4	Chick Challenge	£3.50	❐
0 340 68731 2	Pony Parade	£3.50	❐
0 340 68732 0	Guinea-pig Gang	£3.50	❐
0 340 71371 2	Gerbil Genius	£3.50	❐
0 340 71372 0	Duckling Diary	£3.50	❐
0 340 71373 9	Lamb Lessons	£3.50	❐
0 340 71374 7	Doggy Dare	£3.50	❐
0 340 73585 6	Donkey Derby	£3.50	❐
0 340 73586 4	Hedgehog Home	£3.50	❐
0 340 73587 2	Frog Friends	£3.50	❐
0 340 73588 0	Bunny Bonanza	£3.50	❐
0 340 73589 9	Ferret Fun	£3.50	❐
0 340 73590 2	Rat Riddle	£3.50	❐
0 340 71375 5	Cat Crazy	£3.50	❐
0 340 73605 4	Pets' Party	£3.50	❐

All Hodder Children's books are available at your local bookshop, or can be ordered direct from the publisher. Just tick the titles you would like and complete the details below. Prices and availability are subject to change without prior notice.

Please enclose a cheque or postal order made payable to *Bookpoint Ltd*, and send to: Hodder Children's Books, 39 Milton Park, Abingdon, OXON OX14 4TD, UK. Email Address: orders@bookpoint.co.uk

If you would prefer to pay by credit card, our call centre team would be delighted to take your order by telephone. Our direct line *01235 400414* (lines open 9.00 am–6.00 pm Monday to Saturday, 24 hour message answering service). Alternatively you can send a fax on *01235 400454*.

TITLE		FIRST NAME		SURNAME	

ADDRESS	
DAYTIME TEL:		POST CODE	

If you would prefer to pay by credit card, please complete:
Please debit my Visa/Access/Diner's Card/American Express (delete as applicable) card no:

Signature .... Expiry Date: ....

If you would NOT like to receive further information on our products please tick the box. ❐